CHANNEL

Issue 11 | Autumn 2024

Managing Editor:
Cassia Gaden Gilmartin

Eagarthóir/Aistritheoir Gaeilge (Irish Language Editor/Translator):
Aisling Ní Choibheanaigh Nic Eoin

Published with assistance from Publishing Intern Emily Iseult Duggan.

Published in Dublin, Ireland by *Channel*.
Printed by City Print Limited.

Design and layout by Cassia Gaden Gilmartin.
Cover art by Manal Mahamid.

ISBN 978-1-0686370-2-5
ISSN 2712-0015

Connect with us: www.channelmag.org | info@channelmag.org
facebook.com/ChannelLiteraryMagazine/ | x: @Channel_LitMag |
instagram: @channel_mag

Channel receives financial assistance from the Arts Council.

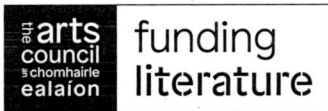

Fiction

Essay

Poetry

Cover Art: *Palestinian Gazelle I* and *Palestinian Gazelle II*, by Manal Mahamid

Palestinian Gazelle I
Etching & aquatint on archival paper
93 x 73 cm, 2016

Palestinian Gazelle II
Etching & aquatint on archival paper
93 x 73 cm, 2016

A note from the artist

As a Palestinian artist working across sculpture, video, and photography, my practice is deeply rooted in exploring the complex intersections between colonialism, identity, and the altered landscapes of my homeland. I use art to confront the ways in which colonial regimes reshape not only human narratives but also the ecological realities of a place. I believe that land, animals, and plants are not passive victims in this transformation; they are active bearers of history, witnesses to the trauma of erasure, and symbols of resilience. My project, *The Palestinian Gazelle*, emerged from these reflections and became a pivotal part of my ongoing exploration of environmental justice and ecological resistance.

The project began with a personal experience at a zoo in Israel, where I noticed a sign at a gazelle enclosure. In Arabic and English, it read "The Palestinian Gazelle," but in Hebrew, it was labeled "The Israeli Gazelle." This deliberate reclassification was more than just a change of words—it was an act of environmental violence, a clear attempt to overwrite a piece of the landscape's story. It echoed a broader policy of naming, erasing, and reassigning identities within the land itself. I realized that the renaming of the gazelle was symbolic of a larger process where even nature is co-opted and redefined by the occupying power. This manipulation of ecological narratives reflects a form of ecological colonialism—where the natural world is altered to reflect the colonizer's claim over the land and its history.

The gazelle has long been an iconic symbol in Palestinian culture, representing beauty, grace, and a connection to the land that predates political borders. But in this encounter, I saw how even the natural world is not spared from colonial narratives that attempt to sever the people's connection to their environment. A later experience in the same zoo deepened the project further. I saw a gazelle with an amputated leg, and when I asked, the zookeeper explained that they had "saved" it by cutting off its limb. This explanation struck me as disturbingly familiar. It reflected the paradox of colonialism: to preserve something by mutilating it, to "save" it by altering it beyond recognition.

From this encounter, the gazelle became a powerful metaphor in my work. To me, the amputated limb mirrors the experience of Palestinians, whose connection to their land has been severed, fragmented, and rewritten. Yet, despite the dismemberment, the gazelle stands, dignified and defiant. It symbolizes the broader fight for environmental justice, where the struggle is not only about protecting land and species but also about preserving cultural identities and historical narratives against a backdrop of systemic erasure.

In creating *The Palestinian Gazelle*, I aimed to highlight how colonial forces not only control human narratives but also manipulate ecological ones. Through video, sculpture, and mixed media, I traced the journeys of the gazelle across a divided and militarized landscape, defying checkpoints, borders, and fences. Running through these terrains, I wanted to capture the absurdity of imposed boundaries on a land that once flowed freely. The act of running became a visual metaphor for resistance: a refusal to accept fragmentation and a reclamation of the land's natural continuity, challenging both environmental degradation and the politics of ecological apartheid that seek to compartmentalize and control movement.

My large-scale sculpture of the amputated gazelle is a deliberate representation of this resilience. Despite its missing limb, the gazelle stands proud—not as a pitiful creature, but as a survivor—a reflection of a disrupted yet unbroken identity. It represents a landscape that, like the gazelle, has been cut apart and claimed, yet continues to endure. By emphasizing the mutilated yet enduring body of the gazelle, I wanted to address the broader issues of environmental trauma—where the land and its inhabitants bear the visible and invisible scars of conflict.

The use of the gazelle in my work is a way of reasserting its true identity—one that is deeply entwined with the history and ecology of Palestine. I am fascinated by how the animal's image appears throughout Arab literature, poetry, and music as a symbol of longing and connection to the land. It is an image that belongs to a time before borders and barbed wire, when the land was whole. In my work, I aim to make visible the tension between what the land was, what it is forced to be, and what it could be if freed from these constraints.

By placing the gazelle in landscapes that span from the north to the south of historic Palestine, I invite viewers to reimagine the land as it once was—continuous, whole, and resilient. I want people to see not just the physical beauty of the gazelle but the broader ecological and political story it tells. This is not just an animal; it is a living archive of a land under siege, a creature caught between survival and loss, and a reminder that even in the face of attempts to amputate its history, it endures.

Through *The Palestinian Gazelle*, I hope to address not only the political erasure of a people but also the environmental and ecological impacts of these narratives. The project is my way of reclaiming the landscape and asserting a form of ecological justice that insists on the inseparability of land, identity, and the natural world. For me, the gazelle's journey is a story of interrupted yet unbroken continuity—an emblem of ecological and cultural endurance that refuses to be confined to the narrow definitions imposed by colonial narratives.

About the artist

Manal Mahamid (1976) is a conceptual multidisciplinary Palestinian artist based in Haifa and Dublin since 2020. Born in Moawia, a Palestinian village, Mahamid has developed a diverse body of work that spans sculpture, video, installation, painting, and photography.

She earned her Master's in Fine Arts at the University of Haifa in 2006, thanks to a scholarship of Excellence from the university. In 2010, she obtained a degree in Museology and Curation from the University of Tel Aviv. In 2024, she completed a Master's in Culture Policy and Arts Management from University College Dublin (UCD).

Mahamid's work has been recognized with numerous accolades, including being shortlisted for the A.M. Qattan Young Artist of the Year Award in 2002. She received the Delfina Foundation's Resident Artist Award in 2007 as part of the Riwaq Biennale, a collaboration between the Delfina Foundation and the A.M. Qattan Foundation.

Her art has been showcased in over fifty group exhibitions worldwide, with notable exhibitions in London, Chicago, Cairo, Dusseldorf, Haifa, Ramallah, Um El Fahim, and Jericho. She also participated in the Qalandiya International Festival in 2014 and 2016, organized by the Arab Culture Association in Haifa.

Mahamid's solo exhibitions include *The Tale of a Gazelle* (2016), *Work in Progress*, and her most recent exhibition *Lines of Flight* in Waterford.

Notes from the Editors

The air, in the moment out of which this issue arises, feels almost too thick to breathe. We're living and working in a present that's heavy with past, laden to breaking point with the consequences of transgressions that stretch back across centuries – runaway climate change; social and economic inequalities along intractable post-colonial lines; and the violence cascading from a lie, sold to a beleaguered Jewish diaspora, of a "land without a people" waiting to be reclaimed.

The ether seems stuffed with questions of how we got here, and how on Earth we can get out. These are the questions that absorbed us as we read through the submissions pile for Issue 11, and in this context it seems no wonder that we arrived at a lineup of work preoccupied with ancestry. Much of the work we chose to publish shows a painful awareness of historical injustice, and of the unspoken social compacts by which we maintain our comfort and our complicity: "By mutual agreement we didn't discuss how we'd stripped flesh or how we boiled it to tallow, how we lit and were still lighting our streets with its renderings," says the speaker of Gemma Cooper-Novack's 'Power' (p.1). Speakers carry a weight of ancestral grief, held in the bones and in the nuances of relationships to land: "There is a memory of cold winters / in my silt", writes Daniel Fuller (p.3). Parents feature prominently: as representatives of old philosophies ill-suited to their children's needs, as absences left by death or distance, and as carriers of knowledge at risk of being forgotten.

There are pieces in this issue that seem to strain against the limits of received wisdom, testing old ways of relating to the world against new problems or seeking to dispense with them altogether. "You forget that the bronze serpent suspended on its pole / might be cheerful about it," says the speaker of Rebecca Bratten Weiss' 'Russian olive (invasive)' (p.22). Brendan Mac Evilly's 'Being and Swimmingness' explores the practice of phenomenology as a way to "peel away learned wisdom, clichés, and preconceived notions … scrape away the filters of ideology" (p. 82). In some pieces, the attempt to see reality anew gives rise to peculiar forms of expression. The syntax can be strange and incomplete, "odd / as an easel moored / to breakwater" (Christine Barkley, p. 72). At the same time, many pieces feature a calling back to long-forgotten ideas in search of insight that might service modern needs. Drawing on ancient Hittite bird oracle texts, David Mullin's 'Ornithomancy' asks "what auguries … from these who by degrees / fail to return in the spring, / or the long-necked birds / that arrive undocumented / too early in the autumn?" (p.76). There is much to admire in the originality of all these pieces, and in their indebtedness to the histories out of which each is inescapably made; in their attempts to reinvent the wheel by increments, even as the wheel supports their collective brave trundle into the unknown.

A recurring concern in this issue is literary ancestry – how to relate to the tangled web of laments, calls to arms, myth and propaganda into which our own words land. Hannah Linden's 'Dear Kafka' (p.65) speaks directly to the ancestor at its heart, hitting him with a sharp critique: "We are saddened to be associated forever with your name". Daniel Fuller's 'All of the Old Poets Used to Write about Nightingales' (p.3), on the other hand, evokes a poetic sensibility or frame of reference to which easy access has, it seems, become cut off. There's ambiguity as to how the speaker feels about what has been lost; the "old poets" and nightingale of the title may be objects of admiration, envy or anger, but what's clear is a fervent desire to speak back to them, and a certainty that to do so will be to split open: "I want to hear the nightingale before I go / and I want to sing back to her in a tender voice", the speaker tells us; "I know it will fracture me, / like the root of an alder". In 'a thing that growls and moans both' (p.112), Paula Dias Garcia's speaker expresses deference to what has already "been said by / the poets the laureates my / betters", but finds room for a crucial act of self-expression anyway. Meanwhile, James Owens' 'One Year After a Summer of Fires' (p.113) questions the efficacy of its own borrowed imagery: "How many stories begin 'at daybreak, the rain …'?"

Such pieces feel at home in a journal of eco-writing, a publication continually re-negotiating its place within a genre that has been defined and re-defined over centuries and within a publishing landscape not always hospitable to ecological thought. With this issue, *Channel* is letting go of parts of itself: our Eagarthóir/Aistritheoir Gaeilge, Aisling Ní Choibheanaigh Nic Eoin, is moving on from her role after artfully shaping the first two years of our work with the Irish language, and this year's wonderful Publishing Intern, Emily Iseult Duggan, is also finishing her time with us. At the same time, with our first single-authored poetry chapbook released this year, the work we do is changing shape. I'm taking my time with the questions this leaves me with: how can I honour the impact that my friends and colleagues have made on this work; how can I take them forward with me? And where do I go from here – what callings has this world shaped, in the particular time-worn contours of its mouth, that myself and *Channel* might do our part to answer?

In making these decisions, the support offered by the words in these pages – the stuff out of which *Channel* is made – is indispensable. For me, there is no greater reward in the work of publishing than the chance to tap into what writers and artists are articulating in their work, no greater guiding light than the strange auguries that the collective unconscious keeps throwing up in our inbox. No greater comfort than to hold a space where we can say together, again and again, "at daybreak, the rain" – in countless variations, in all its inadequacy.

– Cassia Gaden Gilmartin
Managing Editor

It is fitting that I write this final editorial for *Channel* by the sea. Against the grey pallor of a turning season, white foam ridges stand starkly on their waves. The receding tide has left behind it pools of salt water on the road, the only signs of a heavy swell that has now abated. The dips of sand and rock hold in them the memory of each and every tide that has gone before, as well as anticipation of those that are still to come.

This issue is tidal in a similar way, containing threads of past publications, as well as a series of generative ideas which have the capacity to stimulate new work in the future. It is a bidirectional growth seeded in the material of memory, both that which is used to meditate on the past and that which helps us predict the future.

Both the Irish poems included in this issue contain interesting meditations on memory, and curiously, both employ the ocean as a point taken from the linear stream most often dwelt in. Each author creates a space within their work where both the past and future lives of their subjects are visible, but are held in a temporary state of static. In Ellen Harrold's 'Máthair Shúigh Mhór' (p.48), the sea is home to the vibrant and ultimately doomed giant squid that dances in front of the searchlights of marine scientists. In Keev Ó Baoill's 'Más buan mo chuimhne' (pp. 37–39), it is a site of substantial intimacy, uncovering a nascent love developing between a couple as they drink and swim together in Blackrock. These respective moments are briefly frozen for the reader, as we experience the exact points at which the directions of our subjects' lives shift, a divergence that ultimately informs the fabric of their pasts also.

Ó Baoill's poem in particular contains distinct notes of temporal expansion, the many years of a relationship folding out in front of the reader. In this piece the Irish language is boundless, moving freely along with space and time, holding the relationship in its journey; it travels with the couple to a number of countries, adjusting organically to accommodate for the lexical space shared by the two. It becomes a private means of loving expression, as well as a tool used for meaning making. These pieces contain a form of emotional radiance that is rooted heavily in memory, as well as in the very real spatial environment which facilitates the exploration of memory, the ocean.

This is the final issue that I will work on, and it feels apposite that it is with these works I leave you; two poems that are so richly emblematic of the sensibility the magazine tries to nurture. I would like to thank Cassia for giving me the opportunity to be a part of a journal I loved so dearly for such a long time, and for the wonderful friendships I developed in this space. I have no doubt that *Channel* will continue to cultivate a literary environment that inspires the eco-writers among us, and it is with a great warmth that I will watch it grow and develop in the future.

Slán go fóill.

– Aisling Ní Choibheanaigh Nic Eoin
Eagarthóir/Aistritheoir Gaeilge
(Irish Language Editor/Translator)

Dear Reader,

I am writing this, from my home, on a seemingly perfect day— it is calm, there's a silvery breeze, and the window to my left is flooding my desk with crystal winter sunlight. It is still October, but here in Donegal, the seasons are slippery and day-dependent.

I'll let you in on a secret, dear reader, which is that I have been putting off writing this editorial for days now. The reluctance I feel to write a few short lines to sum up a year past, and a year's worth of poignant environmental writing, is certainly not a reflection on my year in *Channel*, which has been wonderful, challenging and empowering. Rather, I realised this morning, I am feeling this reluctance because this past year has been defined, for me, by nightmarish images of a live-streamed apocalypse, and each day that passes is another day that this is still happening.

I am incredibly lucky to be sitting here in Ireland, my life unaffected by violence. I am lucky to have been born here, but luck does not dictate whose lives are taken, assaulted or destroyed by catastrophe; just as genocide is being carried out by Israel with American-funded weapons against Palestinians, the detrimental effects of the Western-accelerated climate emergency will first affect the most impoverished and disadvantaged communities on our planet. The fact that I was born into a privileged country was luck, but the geography of privilege is design.

Creative writing can seem frivolous alongside monstrous political realities; how does a poem or short story coexist with images and knowledge of ethnic cleansing, land confiscation and systematic violence? In some ways, it is totally frivolous. But amidst the videos of unthinkable suffering, I also see videos of resilience and hope. I see a young Palestinian planting seeds into emptied food cans in the Khan Younis refugee camp. I see people cooking meals with what little they've managed to obtain, and sharing them with others around a small fire. I see children making toys from scraps of clothes and food sacks, drawing board games in the sand and kicking bottles into stone goals.

Culture, and its persistence, is an important resistance against the ideologies that threaten our worlds, our environment and our peace. The persistence of art, of food and togetherness, the persistence of the human urge to create and share culture with one another, is powerful in the face of capitalist neoliberalism, global developmentalism and imperialism. While this sentiment is certainly limp in the face of literal bombs and the obliteration of entire families, towns and cities, and meaningful action— active protest and following the Boycott, Divestment, Sanctions movement— must be prioritised, it is also important to bear in mind that art spaces, like *Channel*, are important grounds for the persistence of culture and hope in an increasingly divisive world.

In this issue of *Channel*, among considerate studies of our relationship to the natural world, we have writing that spans and dances through generations, stories of families, and stories that begin after an "end". This brings me back to Palestine; to the slight green sprout of that watermelon plant emerging from the dusty ground of the refugee camp, and the trust that humans will continue to create, even when it seems that the book has ended.

Thank you so much to Cassia, Aisling and all the 2024 contributors and readers for having me at *Channel* this year. It's been a nourishing experience, and I'm so delighted to have been able to contribute to the makings of two beautiful issues.

If I'm to leave you something, dear reader, then let it be this: know that all struggles are connected, and act, in activism, accordingly. There is no environmental justice without social justice, and no social justice without environmental justice. Free, free Palestine.

– Emily Iseult Duggan
2024 Publishing Intern

Emily Iseult Duggan is a writer and chef, living in Donegal. In 2024, she won the New Writing Prize for Fiction at Cúirt International Festival of Literature, and received an Agility Award from The Arts Council of Ireland. She is currently working on her first collection of short stories and participating in The Stinging Fly Advanced Fiction Workshop.

Gemma Cooper-Novack

Power

We woke up and it was raining bones. I should say it was hailing bones. We screamed as they hurtled toward us. I won't say we hadn't seen it coming but you can only be so prepared for a femur to pierce the gazebo roof. What might have been a kneecap took out a child's eye. I want to say we don't know whose bones they were or where they came from, but that isn't true either. By mutual agreement we didn't discuss how we'd stripped flesh or how we boiled it to tallow, how we lit and were still lighting our streets with its renderings. Our homes. By that light we could see what was happening. We were watching an ulna fall so fast it punctured our uncle's lung. We hunkered in porcelain bathtubs while rib after tibia splintered windows. We screamed. We shuddered. We imagined imprints of phalanges where wind had hurtled them against plaster siding and packed dirt. We waited for silence. We knew there were only so many bones in a body. We knew the barrage would stop long enough for us to build a dome, something bulbous that no scapula could perforate again. We'd need fuel to power it.

Daniel Fuller

Caoineadh

they are mowing down the meadows
and the would-be bracken on the riverbanks
last night I dreamt twice that the world was ending
with me still inside of it
and though the grey thrush taps
stories of winters spent on the damp archipelago
of my birth I think I would have preferred
if they were hidden between the tall grasses
and the flowers that make laughter of impressionism
I don't know how I ever thought this time
would be different when everyone here is so serious
and full of the love of oil fields and false cabins
I do not want to be plucked from the mire
I want to scatter myself in it until
I run with the copper stains and the warmth
of generations who did not understand what I held

Daniel Fuller

All of the Old Poets Used to Write about Nightingales

I want to hear the nightingale before I go
and I want to sing back to her in a tender voice.

Somebody will watch me, and I will learn
earnestness beneath the strange green of the oak

while my ashen worries wait for a north wind
to scatter them. I know it will fracture me,

like the root of an alder.
I am a riverbed of loss with an old lilt

through this place. There is a memory of cold winters
in my silt and the tremor

of a time when someone careful drew my form
in different shapes—those that make for a many-folded living.

Now though, the whispers and the last of the moss
are all that bears witness to this conversation—

these last and first of honest words between me
and the nightingale. In the end the rain

takes what remains and carries it away,
southward, leaving me exposed

with all my rotting and dripping—sighing a crónán
into the darkness that recedes with the summer.

Mandy Shunnarah

we love what we long for

What's here is something that we are still building. It's something we cannot yet see because we are a part of it.
  – Mosab Abu Toha, 'We Love What We Have'

Palestinians are siblings to longing & cousins to hope.
I carry the memories of my sedo & taita in my blood & bones.

I touch the tatreez of a thobe against my skin, though I've never worn it.
I feel Sedo's worry beads in my pocket, though I've never carried them.

I feel the Ramallah desert sun on my flesh, though I've never basked in it.
I smell the smoky scent of red poppies, though I've never picked a bouquet.

I sense the oud's plucked notes through the city, though I've never heard a chord. I feel the cool metal key to my grandparents' stone house, razed before I was born.

I taste the oil mashed from family olive trees, though I've never fed upon its nectar. I savor the ripe homeland figs, though I've never tongued the toothsome fruit.

The hope for a free Palestine makes us daydreamers & time travelers.
I yearn for what I fear I'll never have. I long for the simplest of pleasures.

I dream of a bare spot among the poppies, the sun on my face, figs on my tongue, a picnic on the Jordan Riverbank,

& a key in my purse to a home I returned to.

Frances Ogamba

Telepathy

In her final week of life, Chialuka develops a profound need to connect more with the living. The desire prises her apart and makes her clutter her kitchen sink with oddments of food. Gnats fling themselves blindly at the leftovers radiating with rot. A thousand-ant march adorns the walls of the five-roomed bungalow. She does not reach for the insecticide or crush their trail crisscrossing the wall in loops, their mandibles flexing with twigs of food. She sidesteps reddish-brown cockroaches and spiders as if they partner with her in the business of living and there is no distance dividing them at all.

She always wanted her children, Mary and Mike, to visit and warm the house with their voices, and her grandchildren's. Now, the longing wanes, leaving behind only the need to dial their mobile lines and speak with them if the network allows. She needs to talk to them about the new acre of land allocated to their family after the communal land sharing. The rumour that the state government is bringing an industrial farm to their town rattles every lip. Land grabbers will swoop in and steal lands without known guardians. If her children do not know of the anthill looking like a crust of pine needles at the demarcation between Chialuka's land and the next, how will they know what to guard or what to sell when the government comes to procure lands for the farming project?

Her advocacy for the state of Biafra, a region seeking independence from Nigeria, glows from every part of her. The Nigerian government has proscribed the group of separatists. She wishes she knew what levers to pull to make an impact.

A mouse scampers nonstop across the Moroccan rugs covering the floorboards of her sitting room. Another rodent joins the first, and they gnaw through everything: the food in her store, the wood base of the sofas, the sharp-edged toys Mary and Mike were engrossed with in their childhood, which Chialuka has reserved for their children. She doesn't recognize yet what this awl-sharp grief pushing through her nerves means. She darts through her tasks, as if both aware and unaware of the lacks colouring her existence.

Her face bears none of that puffiness of aging. Her flat stomach gives prominence to her rounded hips, which shove outwards like a skin graft. She feels her age in private pains – her blood pressure, which surges and makes her head feel wooly like cotton sometimes, her cavity that often complicates eating, and her joints that catch like a gasp when she makes a sudden movement – but she looks nothing close to sixty-nine.

It is Monday. There is a soft silence around her. The Sit-At-Home order for the release of Nnamdi Kanu, the chief activist of the Biafran dream, shuts down businesses and schools in Eastern Nigeria on Mondays. If she ambles towards the street, it will be hollow of people. Except occasionally when people steal outside to run quick errands and then scurry back to their houses. The tables for street shops lie upturned as if their owners have passed on in their sleep. Every Sunday night, the Sit-At-Home enforcers lay dead logs across the road. Sometimes, they set old car tyres alight, and the char eats into the red soil by morning. The enforcers stuff the air with threats and warnings: *anybody who comes out tomorrow, whatever they see, let them take*. Chialuka imagines their sweaty bodies, lean and muscled, hugged tight by formerly white singlets browned by sweat, shirts thrown across their shoulders like slain game. They remind her of Mike, her son, when he was at that age, and knuckled down to his dreams of getting into a university. But the boys' images sometimes feel like an original, because they stay home and fight for home, and Mike, consistently focused on swapping his hometown and culture for books and white-collar jobs, feels like a reprint. Why can't a child expand into other things and still yearn for home? Must new knowledge breed a resentment of one's origin? Even Mary, older than Mike by three years and with two daughters, invents new excuses each time Chialuka asks her to visit.

Chialuka twists the knob of the FM radio Mary gifted her five years ago. The digital display shows 102.2. The goading voice of a woman jolts her. The woman cusses out business owners who insist on opening on Mondays. The program's stand-in anchor, who assumed the position hours after Nnamdi Kanu was taken by the Nigerian government, interjects his assent to the woman's vituperative attack against insubordination. Chialuka scoops a cupful of raw rice with her right hand, the radio in her left, and strolls to the make-shift coop where her local fowls sleep. The fowls' eyes turn to Chialuka, this owner who only avails them of shelter, but not food. She scatters the grains into the air. The birds continue to stare. Shock maybe. Then the meaning registers. Their wings clap as they peck at the grains. Chialuka chuckles and sprinkles more. She goes into her kitchen and refills the cup and returns.

After the fowls have eaten, she carries a low stool and a basket of ukpaka seeds chopped carefully in uniform square shapes to the centre of the compound. A caller on the radio speaks of an upcoming protest for the release of the incarcerated Biafran activist, which is projected to take place in many towns of the region. The speaker recollects a similar protest, which cut down over sixty young people in Onitsha some months back. *Did we see the news in any Nigerian media outlet?* Chialuka sighs and lowers herself on the stool, careful not to trigger the irritable joints of her knee. She wedges the basket between her legs and spoons portions of the seeds into layers of green leaves that aid their fermentation. She ties up each layer with ropes pared off from the rachis of a palm frond and arranges them in a tray according to their prices. The voices on the radio kindle Chialuka's hopes for the Biafran state. She was sixteen years old in 1967, when Eastern Nigeria first declared itself a new country, Biafra, and Nigeria responded by unleashing war. Her hometown was hidden away in a valley. So, the war reached them as remote sounds of shelling, and increased food shortage because farming exposed people to shells. When Biafra surrendered to Nigeria in 1970, after losing millions of lives, Chialuka remembers weeping alongside her young friends. It's been fifty-three years, and the ache has not died.

Now, her weak knees make her unable to join marches. Her little advocacy is a red and black strip of the flag representing the past republic, which she knots on the stakes of her sales basket while the rest of the flag flutters in the wind.

*

Mary fills the blender with the washed beans and plugs it into the electric wall socket. She is making the girls' favourite meal, the reason they look forward to Monday nights. Their bickering drones in the background as the blender grinds away. Kachi, who is six, is more self-willed than Kene, older by one year and has Chialuka's pale colouring. The girls sneak up on their cat, whom they call bussu, and poke her tail. The cat sneers and charges at them.

"Can you stop bothering the cat?" Mary says from the kitchen. The blender's whine dulls the sharpness of her words, weakens her authority in a way.

Kachi prods the animal again. Kene laughs, clearly entertained by her younger sister's pushback.

"Are both your ears for decoration abi for hearing?"

"It's Kene." Kachi scrunches up her face and pulls her brows together in mock anger. Mary resists the urge to laugh.

"Mummy, it's Kachi!" Kene turns to her sister. "It's you!"

Their fights remind Mary of her own childhood, when she was always shadowed by her parents' instructions even in their absence. She and Mike always fought because Mary envied his privilege as the younger child and the son of the house. Their parents' half-hearted grip set him too loose until he twisted beyond everyone's reach. Each time their mother lumps her and Mike in one pod, each time she says *you both have rejected home*, Mary protests.

Their reasons for not visiting home differ. She, Mary, has two daughters who go to school. The weight of parenting also rests on Mary because her husband, Amadi, works with an offshore firm and claims he is swamped with work all year round, even though Mary has seen hints of another woman. Mike, on the other hand, has only work. Why can't he take a leave and visit his mother? Why doesn't he call or text family?

Mary stirs the bean purée into a bowl and mixes it with cooking spices and water. Then, she uses a soup ladle to pour the mix into small aluminum plates. She stacks the plates in a pot and sets the gas knob on the lowest heat.

A sense of fear arising from an obscure source tugs at her.

"Has anyone seen my phone?" she asks. The girls roll about on the rug in their living room, lost in their own whispers. She finds the phone in a tangle of clothes in the bedroom she shares with the girls. She sits on the mess and dials her mother's number. Their conversation always covers a panoply of topics: Mike's reluctance to marry, Mary's cheating husband and what Mary's decision might be, the recent deaths or weddings in their hometown. Then they argue about the visits. The last time they saw each other was when Kachi was one year old.

"I can't sit that long on a bus. My knees," her mother said when Mary asked her to come instead.

"I can book you a flight?"

"I hate being suspended in the air. Which body will you bury if the plane crashes?" The wind's puff pushed at her voice. Chialuka takes most phone calls outside her house because of the poor network, which has worsened in recent times. Mary always imagines her groping for her footwear and tearing open the door every time her phone rings.

Their video call last week flits into Mary's mind.

"You need a housekeeper. Let's hire someone we can pay."

"Mary, a house help cannot quench the thirst for one's children. Has it not been up to five years since you came?"

Mary stalled. Her mother's guilt tripping came in a variety of phrasings, and every choice caught Mary off guard.

"Even if we come home, we can't live with you. You need someone," Mary said.

Her mother laughed. As always, her infected canine, discoloured at the gumline, an imperfection that flashes at the peak of joy. Every time they video call, Mary sees that dot of black in a sea of white.

"I do all my chores. I don't need help. I only need to see you all and show you the land as well. We will lose that land if you don't know the location," her mother said.

"Why would we lose the land when you are there, Mummy? We will see it whenever we come. Besides, you can keep the land's ownership papers."

"What papers? Have you ever heard that ancestral lands have any ownership papers?" her mother retorted, irritation creeping into her voice.

Now, as she dials her mother's number, a pair of large moist eyes stares wistfully at her from the corner of the bed where Kene and Kachi's clothes are tangled just like their owners when they fight. She digs through the cloth heap with a jittery hand. The eyes belong to the girls' stuffed dog. Fear had already wormed into her. Mary near-laughs at her silliness. She returns her attention to the phone.

She wonders whether her mother was at the market today. Mary discourages her from doing full-time sales. But Chialuka always crafts her refusal with a backstory of how the ukpaka tree chose her as its disseminator; how, as a child, she was mystified by this tree whose fruits were not made of soft pulp, but were shells, long and flat and dangling from the branches like a pair of dead feet; how the shell was an enclosed canoe before she cracked it open and saw a womb housing eight shiny brown seeds. She no longer scours the crannies of their town to buy the ukpaka seeds from the tree owners. She purchases a large quantity of already processed seeds from other sellers and repackages them. Then, she adds a little profit and resells them at Orie market.

How was Monday's Sit-At-Home? she plans to ask once her mother answers. Mary does not care about the Biafran movement. She only asks to make sure that her mother is conscious about safety. Ever since the Nigerian government arrested Nnamdi Kanu, a strange wave of insecurity has strummed the East. Mary intentionally goes tone deaf when her mother strings a speech on how different Biafra will be from Nigeria: free from the reins of corrupt leaders, a new country that will become the Japan and the Dubai of Africa.

Mary dials again with more vigour after realizing that she's been filled with the drift of her own thoughts and paid scant attention to what the network service was saying. Three dots blink endlessly at the end of *calling*. She imagines the trails of connection too slick so that the dots lose their grasp and slip over and over. In the end, her phone toots with a report that the network has failed.

*

Chialuka awakens at dawn to a wind skating over the town. It is still early, but the town already whirs with human noise. Tuesdays are often taut with the need to make up for a Monday spent at home. On her way to the bathroom, a rat scurries towards her and then dashes back the way it came. She snaps off chunks of bread from a loaf and drops them at strategic points. For the rats and the ants and the roaches, and for all the things that will keep the house warm in case she is suddenly unable to pace through it. The chicks congregate on her doorstep as she exits the house, clucking for a repeat performance. She hastens back inside and dips a bowl in the bag of garri in her kitchen. She scatters it in the compound and the ground glistens with the pale white of the flour.

A weak sun floats at the edge of the sky when she closes the compound gate. Commercial bike riders drift towards her as she marches down the road. They ask if she's going to Orie market. They will take her for the cheapest fare, they swear, and will ride gently for the sake of her waist. *Mummy, fine mummy, I carried you the last time.* She'd usually look them carefully in the eye and choose the one who exudes an aura of calm, who would skirt around potholes instead of crashing into them. But it's been a long time since she walked to the market. She's almost forgotten where the road rises in the middle like a hunch, and where it veers off into a sharp bend as if preparing to disappear. She swats the riders away and walks on the road's periphery, taking in thickets that sometimes thin to show glimpses of houses. *Memorize, remember*, her heart chants back at her.

Her stand in the market is a narrow space marked for her amid other ukpaka sellers. The sellers come from different towns but are looped together by the trade. Most of the women are as young as Mary but live inside bodies rendered sturdy and old by the stress of the work. They refer to Chialuka as *Mama*. They often turn to her to resolve disagreements over their rightful spots and poached customers.

She settles into her place.

"Mama," someone calls. It is Uju, thick-bodied and dark brown like the market's sand. Chialuka sometimes sources fresh ukpaka from her.

"Uju nne," Chialuka responds, patting down her long skirt to drape it over her legs.

"You came out late. What delayed you?"

"A lover," one of the sellers interjects. Some of the women laugh.

"Which waist will Mama use to meet the lover? This her waist, just one touch, it will scatter," Vera, a reed-thin seller, says. The vagus nerve at her neck bulges as she crams the banter into the moment.

"Leave my hot Mama alone," Uju says above the racket. "Have you seen her hips? She will court any man she wants."

Other voices join in.

"She's a grandma o."

"So what? Who says the vagina grows old?"

The responses twirl beyond their stand like a coin and touch the nearby stands. Other sellers lean into the conversation, their eyes watering with laughter. Chialuka, who often shies away from subjects of intimacy, feels her organs brim with light, as if she is bursting open. She laughs alongside the women, tells them a brief story of a young man who catcalled her once on her way to the market because he erroneously thought that the flare of her hips must belong to a younger woman.

She dials Mary's number at noon, but the call keeps disconnecting. She will have to try again later. She wants to talk today, while her daughter has time – Tuesdays are Mary's day off work at the Lagos central mall, where she works at the backend of the mall's website: listing products, answering phone calls and online chats from disgruntled customers. They have a discussion pending about Mary's plans to sever her marital link to Amadi, the stout man she brought home to meet Chialuka eight years ago. Chialuka supported Mary's decision even though she voiced her concern about the man's paunch, which seemed stuffed with his ego.

Mary's number isn't going through, so she calls Mike. Surprisingly, she hears a dial tone. She hasn't spoken to her son in weeks because, when she calls, he either answers and puffs like he's on the run and promises to call back, or he does not answer at all. This time, his voice clogs with an unusual dullness.

"Hello, hello." Chialuka worries that the market noise will heighten and disconnect the call. And who knows when another chance will come? She's had this unending sense of panic all week.

She stands inches away from the cackling women.

Voices fill every cranny of the market. Her words do not seem to have enough room to be heard.

"Mummy, how are you?"

She's tempted to accuse him of inattention. Her gripe against him catches in her chest. But the beat of the moment is more urgent. She lingers on the lilt of his voice, how the inflection blurs the first m of Mummy, making it sound like he's saying *ummy*. A speech impediment since he was a child.

"I'm fine. Are you getting enough rest? You sound tired."

She mistakes the new stillness in her ear for her son's pause around her question. Then, she realizes that the network has frozen the call. There is only one service bar on her phone screen when she glances at it. Worry sequesters in her heart.

"Glo is doing system maintenance. The network has been terrible. You are even lucky to make a call," Uju says when Chialuka returns. Customers are already lined up in front of Chialuka's tray.

The foundation of their house was first dug in 1980, the year Chialuka married Mary and Mike's father, Enyi. They squatted with one of his relatives until the walls grew past the lintel level and one of the rooms was covered with a shiny zinc roof that would rust as heavy rains and brazen sun carried out years of onslaughts. The house remained that way and became a landmark for showing strangers the way into their town.

Ehe! Are you seeing a house with a half roof?

Yes! Ana m afu a partially roofed house, should I wait there?

Take a right turn and then a left turn and stop when you see a house that has an incomplete skull.

Enyi worked as a mason, though everyone called him Engineer. Sometimes, he brought home packets of nails and shiny screws and arranged them in one of the empty rooms. They raised their two children in the house while it continued looking like a shoulder sloping from exhaustion.

It was Enyi's death in 1995 that resurrected the house's next phase of construction. The women and men from Enyi's age group were concerned that Enyi had no shelter in his life and couldn't possibly transcend to the afterlife, suffering the same fate. They made donations to Chialuka and the house was draped with a zinc roofing before Enyi's corpse was wheeled into his living room. Mary and Mike, teenagers at the time of their father's death, pushed through life as if making up for what their parents never had. They scaled university education, got jobs that allowed them to save up for the house. They peeled off parts of the house and replaced them with newer parts. A gas stove in place of the kerosene cooker. Cabinets sprang up in the bare kitchen. Iron doors and casement windows plucked old wooden doors and windows from their hinges.

Chialuka thinks of the house as she walks home from the market. She and Enyi made it big enough to accommodate their children and grandchildren. Now, the walls throw back every sound as if the unoccupancy galls them. Still, she feels lucky that her two children, whom some of their kinspeople call too few, are wealthy enough to renovate the house and send her a monthly stipend. Despite their father's early death, never have her children paled; never have they stopped emitting sparks until Mike rose in rank as an accountant and Mary developed content for prestigious companies. Mary at least apologizes and makes bold promises of a time in the future when she shall come with her children. To see her and to see the land. Next year's Christmas. Next two Easters. Chialuka only thinks of the treachery of time and wonders how anyone can boldly make an appointment with it.

She peels off her bra. Her parched breasts flatten on her warm skin. She refuses to hire a housekeeper for this freedom she has, to disclose her breasts to the silence, to scratch the scaly patch of skin under her breasts until the skin tingles. A bell cranks out a harmonious chime inside her head. She uncorks a packer bottle of amlodipine tablets and pops one tablet into her mouth. Her call to Mary has a dial tone, but a child's high-pitched voice fills her ears.

"This is Kachi! My mummy is bathing!"

Chialuka stills, taken unawares by the voice of her grandchild. It feels like an intruding figure, hovering over the unlatched door of her room and tickling the curtains. She suddenly feels too exposed. She grabs a piece of lappa and drapes it quickly over her chest before responding.

"Oh, Kachi, is this you? How are you?"

She rarely gets a chance to speak with the children. They are always either doing schoolwork or stowed away in a room somewhere, playing. Mary constantly talks about them, and this makes Chialuka assume knowledge of them. But now that Kachi's voice rings bright with the dominance Mary often complains about, Chialuka realizes that she does not know who this child is and has no idea how to engage her.

"I'm fine! What is your name?" Kachi asks. Chialuka laughs, her apprehension thawing.

"I am Grandma."

"Oh, Grandma! I know you! You are in our photo album!"

Another voice shushes Kachi. They argue over what is appropriate to say. Chialuka feels the phone changing hands.

"Hello Grandma, this is Kene. My mummy is bathing." It is almost like the first voice, but with a calmer timbre. Chialuka wants to keep them talking because she wants to memorize them talking to her, calling her Grandma, the woman who lived long enough to sire another generation. The girls start bickering about who's held the phone for longer. Their voices thicken into a breathless stream. The line snaps.

Enyi's death sewed Chialuka and her children tight to one another. The disconnection began when they left for university. Their utmost focus became making her comfortable: building a grand house, making sure her bank account was funded enough. "Does money temper abandonment?" she often asks Mary.

*

Mary slumps into her seat and opens the first query box out of the hundreds she must comb through. Her free left thumb swipes open her call history, and she sees her mother's name. A received call. She wonders why her daughters did not mention it. The call did not last up to four minutes. She chuckles at the nature of the conversation her mother might have had with her daughters. What truths did they share in that slit of time?

Femi, her colleague, walks in.

"Hi Mary."

"Femi, good morning."

She returns to her phone, hoping that her pointed expression will communicate her disinterest in holding any kind of conversation. Femi too, either reading the room or not in the mood himself, wheels his chair to his computer. She dials her mother's number as she reads through the first customer's complaint. *Delayed order. Two cases of polystyrene soup containers.* She inputs the order number in the tracking box. There is no dial tone on her call to her mother. She spams several customers with the same messages for their similar cases. *Thank you for your patience as we work on resolving this.* Her heart thrums in the pads of her fingers as she works. She worries about the weakening yarns of her marriage, about her distant brother, and then her mother. They've always spoken once or twice a week, Mary and her mother. Now, her chest throbs with the desire to reach her, to hear her voice.

*

Chialuka stays home on Wednesday and does not make any calls. Her body feels like an animal pelt. She drags herself out of bed and jets food to the fowls. The rats' bloodless beads of eyes feather her heels each time she walks through the house. She crushes breadcrumbs for them. The ants now multiply into a dark expanse. Imagine kinky hair, borderless. She feels an empty fullness that renders food unenticing. But she heats up some egusi soup and sprinkles garri into a bowl of hot water. She has trouble getting the food past her throat. She tries a few swallows, enough to anchor her when she takes her morning dose of amlodipine. She tethers herself to bed all day, listening to the wind chitter through her windows. She hears a knock on the gate and imagines herself as a ghost floating to see who her visitor is. It must be some child sent to buy ukpaka. She knows one such child. He has ashy skin that must take tubs of moisturizer to fix. The knocking stops.

*

The market is a little scanty because of the Thursday protest happening two towns away, at Amichi. People fear that the protest will spill into nearby towns. The army or the police could choose to disperse a crowd with live ammunition. Chialuka shows up at the market with her basket looped with the flag. The ukpaka sellers hail her legendary basket, call her *Biafra Mama*.

"Mama will live to see Biafra!" they sing.

Chialuka still feels weary, but a sense of premonition awakened her this morning, and she felt like pushing herself beyond her body's capacity. On her way to the market, she watched things move by as if half-real or at a great distance and felt herself turn into a spectre as well. The bike riders swooped down on her and offered to take her to the market for free. She was stunned by their kindness. She wondered what they felt for her that her own children had refused to feel. But as the day wears down, the poor network lets in a missed call that must have happened in a void, because it is already one day old. The number has less digits than usual, like an office line that might belong to Mike.

A large crowd of protesters slosh towards the market by mid-afternoon. Chialuka moves closer, to cram full her new curiosity for everything. Most of the protesters are dressed in the colours of the flag. Their faces sheen with those same colours. A group of musicians concealed somewhere in the throng beat gongs and drums and sing in a symphony that moves Chialuka's feet. Wares litter unmanned stands as sellers push towards the drumming and singing. She moves two steps forward and two steps backward. The crowd stops. For her. The women of the market hail her *Mama Biafra!* The crowd takes up the chant. *Mama Biafra! Mama Biafra!* The knots in her head and body loosen. She plies her body to the beat, folding in and out in response to the wild cheers. In the corner of her sight, phone cameras float towards the sky and film her from an angle where they take everything in.

*

"Mummy, I have been trying you all week. Kai! So frustrating! I heard a network mast fell somewhere at Amichi after a heavy wind. I think they fixed it now."

"Yes."

"Are you fine?"

"Yes. I just need some rest."

Her mother's voice sounds like she's slurping water. Mary struggles to make out the words.

"It's the market stress, I guess. I don't know what else we can do to stop you from always going."

"Are the girls awake?"

"No. They are asleep. I wonder what they were telling you the other day. I'm sorry they didn't tell me you called."

"They are wonderful girls."

"You really sound tired. I should let you sleep. Are you taking your blood pressure medication?"

"Yes, yes. Good night, my child."

Mary pauses. *My child?* In her adult years, she has never heard Chialuka speak of her as a child or place any stake of ownership on her. What could be softening up her mother?

"Good night, Mummy." Following up on the oddities of the night, she adds a bit too late because the call has now disconnected, "I love you, Mummy."

*

Chialuka dozes off for a time before she realizes that she's not sleeping. Her heart is clamping shut. The amlodipine tablets are on the low stool by her bed where she keeps bottles of water and medication in case of emergency. She stretches out her hand to reach them, though she also knows that her hands are limp beside her and not engaged in any activity. The rashes under her breasts prickle with sensation and she imagines an artificial hand, clubbed fingers most likely, lifting each boob and raking the nails across her skin until it burns. Her inner body is sagging against her physical body. She feels a mild strain, or pain, as if she's a large button that must squeeze through a tight hole. A penumbral darkness spreads over faces: Mary, Mike, Kachi, Kene, Uju, the bike rider who often wins her over. The yellow sun on the Biafran flag glows at the corner of her vision. She wonders if she should have tidied the kitchen at least. She thinks of the land lying on the other side of town, and how her children's rights to it will dim because of their lengthened absence from home. It is easier to wait for them now that she's as still as a pool. Next year's Christmas. Next two Easters. This lineage of absence she spun with Enyi. Her phone trills endlessly until the rings die off. Just like the knocks on her gate. Someone announces their need to buy ukpaka and gets annoyed at her snobbery.

The seam of silence splinters two days later, on Saturday. The smell reached out to them, voices say. *She's been dead for days, Jesus!* The house crowds with masked faces dashing in and out to draw fresh air. Phone cameras click as people cram their galleries with pictures of her. The police arrive. The town's local security. Morgue attendants. Hands fold and unfold her, drenching her with liquid that hopefully neutralizes the stench. She wonders if they notice her medication on the side stool just out of reach, and the distance she struggled to cover while she sought for it. Sweep! Sweep! Stamp! Stamp! People declare war on all the infestations. Rats and cockroaches scamper into her bedroom, seeking her protection. Sensing her body's looseness, they take off in all directions.

There is a viral video of her dancing at the Biafra protest on the eve of her demise. *Life is but a dream!* voices say. *A healthy and happy woman! Who would have thought?*

Where are her children, someone asks.

Mary and Mike present themselves as if in response to the question. Mary slouches with a weight Chialuka didn't know she had. She looks like she's in physical pain. A ruff of wrinkles scallops the skin under her eyes. Mike's weeping is a clipped sound. Exactly the way he cried as a child. His shoulders quiver as if his body may collapse inwards. She hears her grandchildren, the plash of Kachi's voice and the quiet which Kene effortlessly occupies. Someone bars the children from entering the bedroom.

Chialuka bristles with irritation at her children. See the show she had to put on for them to come. Look at how she made herself gunky to the touch, smudged herself thin, dissolved even. See. See. But they came after all, she reconsiders. She called and they answered.

Annette C. Boehm

An Awk of a Girl

Eons ago, I was so brittle, so long
My hair catching solar flares, my toes gripping bedrock
My arms, my knees: covered in brambles

Don't squirm – hold still – grow granite skin

Like insects, like biblically correct angels,
I've learned to cover myself
in eyes, in hope to startle those who would eat me

Annette C. Boehm

Untethered

Battery packs from the ISS are expected to hit
the atmosphere, create a sonic boom, burn
up well before the surface. I watch
another movie where meteorites cause
an extinction level event, which makes everyone
clear, we can see what's under those
same-same blank faces. The troubled hero
makes it, saves his wife and child, and walks
into the blinding sunlight once the ashes settle.
I envy them. Maybe that's what it would take:
an almost-reboot. A chance to build something
new, something liveable. If one is the hero
of the story. Or his wife. Or child.

Rebecca Bratten Weiss

Russian olive (invasive)

You forget that the bronze serpent suspended on its pole
might be cheerful about it. You've grown accustomed
to seeing everything in shades of dead sparrows on doorsteps,
hearing all the music in the key of blood on lintels, loving
only the ones who are trapped in stone, full fathom five.

All winter, you've thought of the serpent as hungry, the
hunger you get when you know you'll never eat again.
You've considered how some mammals are venomous,
and thought, good for them. You'd sharpen the tooth of the
cobra if you could. You'd send it a file baked in a mouse.

When you were small, your house caught fire. In the truck,
you watched as red tongues licked the walls, while the sky
rained ash and Bibles, and birds exploded into flame.
Then, shattered glass. Your dad's head at the window,
your rocking horse flying through the air, a thing with wings.

Now you see the serpent sunning itself. Eyes half closed.
The walk to Gehenna is not long. You can talk to the dead
and to the living, too. You can tell them, "Today, I heard a
new song. Bluegrass. Fiddles. Thought of you." Outside,
the air is full of flowers. Not all of them are poison.

Rebecca Bratten Weiss

On New Year's Day

Maybe it wasn't so beautiful, that life,
but we loved it, the air rank with cowshit, cliffs
bleeding coal, ponds red like infection.

No one was talking yet about the earth burning,
but sometimes in the evenings we saw fires
in the canyons, tasted burning tires.

And one New Year's, it rained all night and
the streams became rivers. The next day
we went squelching, wading, swimming.

And how happy we were, happy among leeches,
happy when we found the carcass of a deer, stripped
hairless, bloat-white in the water.

Happy to drag the dead thing from the mud,
hack its head off, walk up the muddy road,
clutching dead antlers, faces streaked with mud.

And I was a goddess, the world at my feet and
my knife at its neck. I was Artemis, not yet vengeful,
happy to flash my thighs for hunters, in the warm night.

And we loved it all, drank it in the way the deer,
descending from gray hills, drank in the deep water,
not hearing the rush of the coming floods.

Rebecca Bratten Weiss

Heron Slut

In the park everyone is perfect but the heron slut,
long-legged and hungry, solitary in the shallows.

Everyone is perfect and white and gleaming,
even the trees, streaked with birdshit.

Perfect and white, the grass beneath the heronry
is ghost grass, dying like the rest of us.

The grass beneath my feet doesn't even bend
as I walk through the park, past careless lovers.

Beneath my feet graves show their teeth, above,
the heron slut shits in her white nest.

Graves show their teeth, white like shit streaks
on perfect trees, devouring all that we love.

White like shit the perfect people languish
in the grass, tiny mouths open to devour.

The perfect people do not see her as she passes,
long-legged, collecting her smooth prey.

People do not see my nest in the pale trees,
my mess of a nest filled with favorite things.

See my nest, here my treasures, tiny bones
of days shattered by hunger and haste.

Here my treasures, men I loved, bones
white slender knives, names forgotten.

Men I loved, days I shattered, ghost grass
twisted in coils, dying like the rest of us.

Tess O'Regan

Misty, or Vanishings of Unclear Origins

She has been in the family longer than he has, since before Odhran was born. Before her they had her sire, and his sire before him. She was the first horse he ever sat.

We do not deal in ponies, Da said—Bruce being the only exception, and Ma had not yet bent that rule to get him—so they put Odhran on Mystic. She was young herself and energetic, but she must have known by the weight of him that he was precious cargo, because she went slow and was always gentle. For years she was the only one he would ride. Around and around the lonely tree in the paddock and then, when he was older, down to the beach where she was not slow and not gentle but raced smooth like a raven slicing through wind. When she foaled late in the spring before secondary it came as a surprise. Odhran stood in his confirmation suit and watched her labour, but Ma ushered him into the car before the foal came. He never saw it. The body arrived, but the soul did not, and it went straight into the ground with the placenta. Mystic never recovered.

It did not ruin her. She was still gentle and smooth, but when she went slow it was not because she chose to. He took to riding another horse, and for years she only went out in the mornings before school, when he let her roam freely beside Bruce, searching out the fresh dew in the paddock. For years that was all she did. He finished secondary and went off to college and pretended to go to classes and, when he failed his exams, he came home.

That was an expensive holiday son, Da told him, but he did not tell him it was a mistake.

The stable hands talked though, said it was a waste of money they did not have. The day after Odhran heard them, he went to Da and asked to open a school. It did not matter then that Mystic was slow, because slow meant safe. He put the small ones on her when they came, and she was as careful with them as she had been with him. Until today.

*

The first real day of sun. The warm stuff. The stuff that filters out the blue and leaves it soft in the shadows, glazing the rest of the world gold. Odhran sucks the last lungful from his fag and flicks the butt away. Under the menthol sits the sweet smell of horse manure and freshly cut sawdust and the cocktail is not unpleasant. He exhales and pushes off the wall. Leaves the pool of sunshine empty behind him save for a steaming cloud of smoke, arcing this way and that in the still air. He is halfway across the farmyard when he hears the scream.

It rises from the covered arena before him like shrill birdsong, and it is followed immediately by an off-pitch whinny. He does not run, although he should. The arena was once a barn, but now its corrugated iron walls have been cut out at the sides so only a roof and supports remain, and anyone passing by can look into its carcass. If anything was really wrong he would be able to see it from here. But inside the arena nothing moves. From this vantage there is only sun-hazed air and tossed-up bedding where the horses have trod.

Stillness. He reaches the gate, pulls back the bolt, pushes through. The half-walls fall away, the panorama of the arena opening up before him. Stillness alright.

The child is crumpled on her side, face mushed into the soft dirt, a mix of cac and wood shavings and the odd bit of straw for drainage. He cannot see her eyes or know if they are open; the cap of her hat is titled down, like those of the criminals he sees on telly, hiding her face. She is wearing a chest-protector too, that makes her look like a box, her legs and arms too small to throw the shape. She is no more than seven.

Then movement: one thin pointed elbow kicking out in reflex. He unsticks, and the dirt beneath him disappears until it becomes the dirt beneath her, and he is kneeling in it and hovering over her and fixing her cap and not knowing what to do, and then she is rolling onto her back and blinking up at him, all confusion and frowning when she wakes enough to feel the hurt. She begins to cry.

He calls the ambulance and then the parents, but the parents get there first.

We were in the area, the father says, still hunching over the wheel even though they are standing in the yard.

Where is she? The mother asks and does not wait for an answer.

She finds her in the shed, but has to wait for her eyes to adjust before she can make out her chicken on the single chair inside.

She won't speak. You say the horse threw her? She looks back at Odhran, lurking in the doorway. She clucks. Have you no first-aid kit, her palms are all scraped up and– shh, yes I know baby—I think her arm is broken.

The father nudges his glasses up his nose, nervous like. Who do we have cover with? He takes out his phone.

Cover? No, don't call the bloody insurance company, Jack, have you no sense? Get an ambulance. Hey, it's okay baby, just sit back and—okay, I'm here. Mummy's here.

I've got an ambulance on the way. Odhran eyes the child. Clinging to her mother, hiding in the folds of her long cardigan, she is young and upset and silent. Wet eyes blink back at him, unfocused and slightly wild, and there are three roses blooming on her face, one on each cheek and her chin. Her teeth chatter, trapping her tongue behind them with the threat of being bit through.

An adrenaline dump—those wear off, and kids like to talk.

There's wipes in the glovebox. No. Not you. Odhran halts mid-step, turns back to the family in the shed, but the woman is looking at her daughter. I want to hear it again.

The father flees to the car and all is quiet but for the occasional sniffle. Odhran rocks on the balls of his feet, pats himself down until he finds the pack in his front pocket, then stops. The woman's eyes glint at him from inside the shed. He crosses his arms and surrenders his post at the door, joins her in the dark.

Tell me again.

The horse threw her. Behind the woman, the girl studies the floor. Wooden and unpolished; scars of sawn-off branches stare back like a hundred lidless eyes. I looked away for a second and she was on the ground.

How long was she out?

I don't know, maybe two—

Tell the truth. What happened? There is not enough light to see her face. Tell the truth and I won't call my lawyer. Why won't she speak?

I told you the truth. The horse—

Misty left. I was on her back and then … then I wasn't. She disappeared. The child keeps staring at the floor, but reaches out to the hat on the apple box next to her and pops the cap down.

Ciara! Thank God. A weight slips off the woman's shoulders and she goes with it to her knees, looking up at her child like an idol. I thought you'd lost your voice.

It's Mystic, Odhran says.

What?

Her name is Mystic, not—

And then, heralded up the drive by its siren, the ambulance. Its red and blue lights flash through the trees like tiny gems. They take her out of the shed on a stretcher, although she is not that busted up and could walk the distance herself. Odhran leans against the wall as the paramedics check her over. The mother does not spare him another look before loading in beside her daughter and disappearing down the road. The father lingers and shuffles up to hand Odhran his card.

I'd say we'll be in touch shortly, he offers. And then: you'll have to do something about that horse.

The car kicks up dust in its wake. The gravel is loose and fine and before long the car cannot be seen through the powdered fog. Odhran breathes in but the air is sharp and empty. He pats himself down again, finds his fags and lights up. He lets his head fall back on the first pull and stays like that, staring up at the blue sky for as long as he can, then shuts his eyes against the world. Listens to the silence, and moves to find her.

*

The paddock is empty but for the old shetland Bruce, as is the stableyard. There is no one in the tack room except the dog who follows him into the feed room, but that too is quiet, and only the stallion in the stall beside breaks the silence, snorting softly when Odhran passes without offering an apple.

The door to Mystic's stall is still open from when he led her out. Inside it is like a cave, warm and damp, the air dripping with the wet ghost of her breath. She is not here. He did not think she would be, but he does not know where else to look. His first friend, and still he does not know where she would go. Somewhere in the rafters a pigeon coos. It is a symmetrical sound, well balanced, two hoots on either side, and it fills the space around him. But everything must end and when it does, he misses the clang of the farm. He should not have given the hands the day off.

The dog finishes his business at the door frame and comes to sit at Odhran's feet, craning his neck to show him the whites of his eyes.

There's a boy, Odhran tells him but forgets to pat his head. He is thinking he should muck this place out. It smells of piss and sweat; the straw is not doing its job. Someone left a shovel leaning against the wall outside, and he takes that and a brush from the tack room and before the sun has passed its zenith he has scraped out the wet slop. He brings in the fresh bedding with a creaking rusted wheelbarrow and tosses the stuff around until it lies even, but still after all that there is no horse to put away.

A deep breath. A sigh. He goes to the paddock fence and threads his legs through, sits watching Bruce munch through daisies.

Yesterday, Ma took her coffee here and had hummed through half of 'Born to Run' before Da brought the radio down. Hold your whist woman, you're butchering it. And that got her singing, keeping time in her smoke-scarred voice with the scratched CD they kept meaning to replace. You'll be fine, won't you? Da asked under Clemons' sax, and Odhran said he would be. Alright, he said, and passed the boys' pay over, and Odhran took the wadge and put it in the breast pocket of his denim jacket, a compact rectangle like a second pack of fags.

He wonders where Mystic's run off to, and how long it'll take for things to fix themselves, and then he wonders how long he's got until the phone rings.

*

TESS O'REGAN

He picks up the second time and says nothing until the whiny voice on the other side says: Hello? Hello? four or five times, and then he says: Who's speaking please?

Is this Eoin Mahon?

Mac.

Right, Mr—

And it's Odhran. I'm Eoin's son, Odhran. Out the kitchen window the sun is falling beneath the horizon and all the grass and concrete and dirt that bathed in gold not an hour ago lights up blood red under stratus clouds that stretch the length of the sky, purpling like fresh bruises. Odhran cannot see past the trees at the edge of the paddock; the landline, still attached to the wall, won't give him reign to look. He asks again: Who is this?

Sorry, Odhran. I'm the Briggins' lawyer, Mr Holden. I'm calling about the incident that occurred this morning? Papers shuffle in an office somewhere far away. Odhran, standing empty-handed in the kitchen, winds his fingers through the phone cord, twisting the curling rubber around and around.

You mean what happened with the little girl?

Ciara. Yes, I do.

It wasn't serious, she was fine afterwards. Up and talking in no time.

Not everyone involved feels the same way.

The dog makes a rumbling sound and sits up and cocks his head. Odhran calls him to heel with a click of his fingers but the dog does not move.

How's that?

Ciara has a mild concussion and two broken bones, Mr MacMahon, she's currently under observation at the hospital and will probably be in all night.

Huh. The dog stands up and turns in a circle, crosses to the back door and paws it, nails hissing against the wood. Odhran cringes, steps away from the phone to unlock the door.

Yes, it's been a terrible worry for her parents but she'll be alright, that's not why I'm calling. Mr MacMahon, are you listening?

Odhran scoops the phone off the kitchen table where he left it.

Yeah, I'm here. He left the door open in his hurry to get back and the evening chill bites through the air. So why are you calling?

The Briggins don't want to have to get the insurance people involved. They don't want to make this harder than it has to be, they know your business has been in a spot of trouble recently.

Right. His father has not mentioned any such spot of trouble and neither has his mother.

The man on the other side hesitates before he speaks again. Odhran, is your father there by any chance?

He just went out. But I'm his business partner, you can say to me whatever you've got to say to him.

Another hesitation and another flick of paper. Yes, I can see that. What age are you, son?

Nineteen.

Air down the phone as if the man has breathed right into the receiver. Old enough. Well, like I said, they know you don't want to be getting the insurers involved and they're fine with that but—

That's good.

But—the man does not sound like he takes kindly to interruptions—they do want compensation for their daughter's injuries. Call it reparations. A beat while the man on the phone waits for Odhran to say something, and Odhran waits for the man on the phone to continue. The man on the phone continues. They've come up with two forms of payment and they wanted me to communicate them to you.

Another beat. What are they?

Well, a cash payment wouldn't go amiss. Call it something like ten thousand even and they should back off.

Ha. Silence on the line. That's ridiculous, she fell off a horse! Kids take tumbles all the time. She's fine.

Usually when they do that they do it at a registered riding school. With insurance against these things.

Out the window, the branches of the younger trees blow in the wind and a strange bird calls, guffawing in the early night when all the rest have gone to roost. The kitchen door is still open and the air raises goosebumps on his arms.

Are you blackmailing me? The birdsong cuts off when he speaks and he realises it was not birdsong at all but his own laugh.

Mr MacMahon, I am a member of the Law Society of Ireland, I assure you this is not—

What's the other option?

Mr and Mrs Briggins are willing to bring this to the courts if the matter cannot be settled privately. They suspect they might have a case for negligent behaviour.

How's that?

They have reason to believe you were not immediately at hand when Ciara was thrown off the animal, nor do they think you were even in the same building.

And what do you think?

I think you have another option.

Odhran waits him out.

The animal.

Mystic. What about her?

They think she's wild. Too dangerous to have around children.

Mr Holden. Words can hang heavier than a dead man from the gallows when you know you will not like what follows, but Odhran drags them out of himself regardless. What's the other option?

Put it down. It goes to sleep by Friday and this whole thing goes away.

*

The phone slides back into its cradle with a ring. Across the kitchen, the door remains ajar. Odhran goes and stands in it, whistling for the dog, but the dog does not come. The lamp outside on the wall burns bright and buzzing, but against the vast expanse of the blue dusk it is nothing.

Dark swallows light and takes his whistling with it as an added snack, spits back a chill in exchange. He pats himself down, searching for a cigarette. It will not do much to heat him but some things are about the symbol rather than the actual effect. He does not find the pack but, in his hunt, he finds the money. Still in his breast pocket and neatly folded once over; not much but enough to reimburse a weekend away.

He gets an envelope from the bottom drawer. It is bright blue and has his name on the back from a birthday long passed, and it is empty, and the seal is still good. He puts the money in, crosses out his name, writes *MA* and *DA* underneath. Then he licks the seal and closes it. He leaves it dead in the middle of the table and it lies there even now.

*

The dog is not in the stable yard or the tack room or even in his favourite corner under the shed. Mystic's stall, although still open, houses nobody, equine or canine. Odhran checks the open air arena but it is as empty as it always is when his mother is away. So too is the glasshouse. He does not need keys to peer in and see that. It is as dark inside as it is out and he carries no torch because he forgot to get batteries at the shop, yet he knows the dog is not there because there is no flash of white, only grey and blue and more grey as the blue dies away. The moon shines on nothing.

But it shines nonetheless. On the long grasses of the paddock, the ones by the fence that Bruce has not gotten to yet, and on the split log that has been left as a jump in the middle of the field. On the lonely tree, the sole survivor of what was once a forest, standing regent over it all, and on the cluster of mist underneath the tree's branches. All of it glints silver in the grey. The dog sits in a shadow by the gate. He is silver too, in parts, black and silver where he should be white, and he does not come when Odhran calls. He looks up and around, and he waits for Odhran to join him, so Odhran does.

What are you doing boy? The dog leans into his hand but makes no sign of standing. He points his nose into the paddock, ears falling back like he smells something that is not right. Odhran follows his gaze. The enclosure is empty. He brought Bruce back to his stall hours ago. There is nothing, only fog.

But that is not right. It is a dark night but mild, late spring, and the moon is out. There should be no fog. Yet there it sits behind the tree, so dense that he cannot see through it. It is just the right height to conceal a horse.

When she steps forward, smooth and graceful, the white air clings to her as if it does not want to let her go. It forms a film over her coat and, when it dissipates, the colour becomes absolute. A shadow. The night would swallow her if the moon were not so bright. Her coat was never dark, she was born white and greyed over the years, yet she is dark now. If it were not for the carriage of her head or the peculiar way one ear twitches before the other catches up, she could be another horse.

She turns her head to stare across the field, and muscles bulge as her left side comes to face Odhran and the dog. There amidst the unblemished tone of her coat sits a spot. It is small and irregular and white, and it catches the moon at an angle so that it glares in a blaze of blue fire. Nothing beside remains.

Mystic! Like the dog before her she does not come when called. Unlike the dog, she does not wait for him to approach. The word flies through the silence but it does not reach her.

Gone. Away over the fence to her left, down past the stableyard with the tack room and the feed room, past the stalls where the other horses sleep, until she passes her own stall with its door still swinging and the pigeons' coos vibrating within the stone walls, and she hesitates but goes on her way, to the farmhouse and its open back door and further until she is shrinking, shrinking, a toy horse on the horizon line.

He does not let her disappear. He cannot catch up but the gap between them will not grow as fast if he runs, and so he does. The dog tears after him, howling, a train of three carriages pursuing one after the other and, with the ring of hooves, the slap of feet, the crack of a bark, the farm becomes as loud as any station. An evening chorus to break the day's silence.

He crashes onto the lane behind the house, hidden in spurts of overgrowth and japanese knotweed and nettles that tear at his face, his arms, his legs as he battles by. The path is more forgiving to the dog. His muscles weave like long grass in and out of the branches with such ease that he soon overtakes Odhran and reaches the crossroads. He pauses, swings his head to either side, but there is no scent.

When Odhran emerges, bloody furrows cover his cheeks like cat scratches and his breath is gone and there is no sign of her. The dog looks at Odhran, despairing brown eyes glinting in the night, then he throws back his head and laments.

It's alright. You don't have to come any further. He leaves the dog at the border between lane and beach, slipping down the side road to the left, down the steep mud path, losing his footing and sliding for real now, falling, stumbling to the end of the slope.

On pebbles and coarse sand and seaweed, she stands and she waits. She is barely visible now, barely audible. The dark sea pulls at her, or maybe she pulls at it—a black hole devouring everything around her—and its whispering crash and retreat steals her snorted breath from the air.

Only the bright spot on her neck shines out. Yet somehow she holds Odhran's gaze with her own, somehow they know when the other nods, and he knows she is years younger and she knows he is nearly a man grown. She knows she is loved and he knows that he cannot help. All these things they know fall sheer and choking over the beach. But it is not enough to stop him from moving when she does, running where she runs, chasing her into the waves, water soaking his jeans and weighing him down, salt sucking at his skin.

He cannot match her, cannot go as deep. Feet, calves, thighs, groin, waist, chest. The water meets the same points on both of them but he is shorter, taken faster. She looms in front of him, an invisible presence, black coat against a midnight sky. Then something trips him and he stumbles and when he looks back she is gone.

On the surface a froth bubbles, churns, forms a circle and begins to steam. It rises, dancing white streams twisting in and out of each other. But that cannot be seen from afar. From afar there is only this: a fluke of light glinting in the night that could, if you squint, look like something to navigate by.

Keev Ó Baoill

Más buan mo chuimhne

Más buan mo chuimhne,
    bhíomar cois cladaigh sa Charraig Dubh
      (muid cairde amháin ag an stáitse seo)
        agus muid beirt pisín ólta

Más buan mo chuimhne,
bhíothas ag múineadh roinnt bheag Gaeilge duit—

*   ispíní, sceallóga, sciob sceab,*
*   sceitimíní, agus mar sin de*

Más buan mo chuimhne, thaitin an focal *ispíní* go mór leat, an fhuaim bhog
    es sin ag impigh
orainn a bheith níos cúinne agus muid ag rámhaille leis an ól istíoche

*   an oíche úr sin*

Is dócha gur thaitin an focal sceitimíní leat don fáth céanna,
    an fhuaim bhog esach sin, an fhuaim bhog sin a bhí ag teachtaireacht
      linn freisin
    ón bhfarraige thonnach ós ár gcomhair

An é sin a bhí ag tarlúint an oíche úr sin? Agus muid ar meisce, cois cladaigh,
    ag gáire go cúthalach lena chéile,

      An é go raibh sceitimíní ort? Nuair a d'éirigh tú, gan choine,
        'is tú ag siúil uaim i dtreo na farraige,
      fonn práinneach ort do bhraon a scaoileadh

An raibh an fhuaim bhog *esach* sin ag impigh ort an teannas eadrainn a
    bhrise? An raibh an
fharraige do do mhealladh uaim? An raibh sibh ag suirí lena chéile?

Ar thuig sí cad a bhí le teacht? Ar thuig an fharraige dáchreidte, thonnach
   sin nach cairde
amháin a bheadh ionann gan moill? An raibh sí ag pleidhcíocht linn? An
   dóigh leat gur
theastaigh uaithi an teannas grámhar sin eadrainn a leathnú ar feadh
   tamaillín beag eile?

Blianta ina dhiagh sin, agus muid ag siúl go seolta i gcathair i bhfad ón
   bhfarraige sin—nuair
      nach cairde amháin a bhí ionann a thuilleadh ach *lover boys*, mar a
         ghlaodh orainn go
         húrghránna ar an tsráid, nó péire *"lezzie girls! so beautiful!"*
mar a d'fhógair stráinséir aerach eile, go dearfach, agus muid ag trasnú
   an bhóthair uair éigin
eile—cé go raibh muid ag gáire go méar, ag suirí lena chéile sa chathair
   sceitimíneach sin,
d'airigh an fharraige shuaimhneach sin, Muir na hÉireann, go mór
   uainn beirt

Blianta ina dhiagh sin fós agus muid ag teastail ar an Ubahn, an U-acht,
   (an Ú a hOcht mar a
bhíodh muid ag glaoch air go magúil) i mBeirlín—cathair thartmhar eile
   i bhfad ón
bhfarraige—táim fós do do mhúineadh, ár gcúpla focail á labhairt eadrainn,

> *mo ghrá thú,*
> *a ghrá mo chroí,*
> *go cinnte, go cinnte*

You'd miss the sea though all the same,
wouldn't you?

> *Ó go cinnte, go cinnte*

Mo ghrá thú, mo ghrá thú

Aireoidh sí uaim go cinnte,

mo ghrá thú, mo ghrá thú

Más buan mo chuimhne, theastaigh uait dul ag snámh an oíche úr sin,
   agus an fharraige sin
scaobach, na tonnta ag brise in aghaidh na clocha

Más buan mo chuimhne mheisciúil, bhíomar in ann na tonnta a mhothú
   ar ár gcraiceann,
sprae na farraige dár magadh,

Amhail is go raibh sí dár gceistiú—

> *Nach ceart díbhse a bheith*
> *imithe abhaile faoin tráth seo?*

Agus fós, *a ghrá mo chroí*, theastaigh uait snámh inti

Más buan mo chuimhne,
         bhí faitíos orm
'is tusa, *ó mo ghrá thú*, chomh calma!

Is dócha, *a ghrá mo chroí*, go raibh
         faitíos ortsa freisin

                  an oíche úr sin,

Nach *sceitimíní* amháin a bhí i gceist

               tú faitíosach roimh a bheith ceanúil liomsa,
            'is an fharraige do do mhealladh go sceitimíneach,

         'is faitíos ormsa dul a' snámh

Keev Ó Baoill

If memory serves

If memory serves me
    we were by the shore in Carraig Dubh*
        (us just friends at this stage)
            and us both pissed drunk

If memory serves me,
I was teaching you a little Irish—

sausages, chips, free for all,
excitement, that kind of thing

If memory serves me, you liked the word *ispíní* a lot, that soft s sound begging
us to be quieter and us rowdy with drink

that night

You must have liked the word *sceitimíní* for the same reason,
    that soft *s* sound, that soft sound that was coming to us also
    from the waves on the ocean in front of us

Is that what was happening that night? Us drunk, by the shore, laughing
    shyly with each other

    Was it that you were excited? When you rose, without finishing,
        and walked away from me towards the sea,
    urgently needing to relieve yourself

Was that soft *s* noise begging you to break the tension between us? Was the
sea drawing you from me? Were you flirting with one another?

Did she understand what was going to happen? Did that unbelievable,
  billowy ocean understand
that we would not only be friends? Was she messing with us? Do you
  think that
she wanted that loving anticipation between us extended for a little
  while longer?

Years after that, us walking in a city far from that sea—when
           it wasn't only friends we were anymore but *lover boys*, as we were called
           maliciously on the street, or a pair of '*lezzie girls! so beautiful!*'
as another queer stranger said encouragingly while we crossed the road—
even though we were laughing and flirting with each other in this exciting city,
we both missed that calm sea, the Irish sea.

Years after that again and us travelling on the U-bahn, U-acht (the Ú a hOcht
as we jokingly called it) in Berlin, another thirsty city far from the
sea—I am still teaching you, our *cúpla focail* spoken between us,

                              you are my love,
                              the love of my heart,
                              go cinnte, go cinnte

You'd miss the sea though all the same,
wouldn't you?

                                        Ó go cinnte, go cinnte

My love, my love

                                   I'd miss it for sure

My love, my love

If memory serves me, you wanted to go swimming that night, the sea
choppy, hissing—the waves breaking against the rocks,

If drunken memory serves me, we could feel those waves against our skin,
the sea spray mocking us,

As if asking—

> Shouldn't you both be gone home
> by now?

And even then, my love, you had to swim.

If memory serves me,
        I was afraid,
and you, *my love*, you were so brave.

I am sure that you were
        also afraid

                that night,

That it wasn't just *excitement*

        you afraid of being affectionate with me,
        the sea luring you in excitedly,

        and me afraid to swim.

*Blackrock

KEEV Ó BAOILL

Helen Chen

Morning Routine

I raise the blinds
puddle of sun
light laying down
on the table a trail
of heat, I brush
my teeth and spittles
blur my edges, outside
a woman and kid
syncing their steps
pigeons suddenly
ascend, Red
lipsticked girl
in the mirror pose
back to me, same time
I take the bus, it takes me
everywhere someone is
going, light passes
through my body
leaving shadows
on the floor above me
the sky wears
a dress of clouds

Erin Wilson

The Understory in Autumn

The creature
that moves
through the woods
towards you
with a brass candle snuffer,
putting tree after tree after tree out,
is Death's sister.

~

Death's best friend
is a bent bow,
strung with grief-gut,
playing
a charred fiddle.

~

Death's dog
is deaf,
blind,
dumb
and toothless,
but is adept
at retrieving
thrown bones.

Four legs, yes,
and comes when it's called.
Its fur is grizzled tar.
But otherwise
it looks
like a paroxysmal maggot.

~

Death's aunt
lives
in the attic
of your mind
ceaselessly
knitting
a grey sweater
with the whorled grey yarn
whose source is
the fastidious
uncoiling
of your mind.

When she is done,
where will you be?

[A flake of embryo
floats
in amniotic fluid,
awaiting
its clothing.]

~

Just after
pushing
Death out,
Death's mother
bore down
once more
to force a second child,
a stillborn.

It still hangs,
swinging
like a hundred pound raisin,
from her wizened right breast.

~

Death's grandparents
are authors
who tirelessly
unwrite
every word
ever written
by holding a mirror to
the image
of their straw hands
moving
through air.

~

Death
is the blackest stone
that does not exist.

Fawn Emmalee Ward

Silent/Sounds

White noise. The ocean soliloquies nearby,
crescendoing over broken rocks while high tide
breathes soft and unending from under.
White light reflects every length of wave,
this is not unlike the shore.

Matsutakes in the sand. Obscured
by needles and weeping moss, resonating tones
in some long language beyond the pace of human ears.
White veils swaddle gills that do not breathe.

Snow falling is not silent
but who can tell you how it sounds?

Ellen Harrold

Máthair Shúigh Mhór

Rud aineoil
Ag casadh timpeall sa dorchadas go taitneamhach
Máthair Shúigh Mhór
Ag lonrú
bithcheimiceach agus beo os comhair na ceamaraí taighde.
Lá éigin
éireoidh tú tríd an uisce –
i dtreo gathanna na gréine.

Scaobfar isteach inár mbád thú agus craolfaimid
an t-ionad.
go dtí nach bhfuil tú chomh tábhachtach 's mar a bhí
agus tá an corp atá agat
curtha i dtalamh nó tine.

Ellen Harrold

Giant Squid

Unknown thing
Dancing sensually in the dark
Giant squid
Shining
biochemical and alive in front of the research cameras.
One day
you will rise through the water –
towards rays of light.

You will be scooped into our boat, and we will carry you across
    the airwaves
to the centre.
until your importance dwindles
and your body
is placed in earth or fire.

David Ralph

Marginal Soils

The sheepfarmer in the hills outside the city had been reluctant to sell the dog to Frank. The sheepfarmer believed working dogs should be out on the land and not coddled indoors in cities. But the sheepfarmer had a litter of twelve black-and-white border collies, he couldn't find homes for them all, so in the end he let the pup with the most peculiar white markings across its face leave with Frank. The markings, zigzagging here, protruding there, looked like the map of some strange territory.

Back in the city that first night in Frank's small house, the dog whined when he went upstairs to his bedroom. After a few moments of this, Frank relented and let her up into the bed with him. Frank didn't want to get her into bad habits, but he'd just taken the dog from her mother after all, he could make this small concession for one night. A month later the dog—who by now had been named Angy—was still sleeping in the bed with him. Frank had to admit it. He liked having her there at the foot of the bed when he woke in the mornings. He liked having her follow him round every room of the house.

It was only once Frank and Angy were outside the house that their problems began. The vet Frank had taken Angy to for her vaccinations outlined such a bewildering multitude of hidden dangers. Worms, parasites, ticks, fatal fleas lay in wait wherever they went. Infections, influenzas, coughs, viruses lurked everywhere. As little as a stray sniff of the dog's snout off the wrong surface could prove catastrophic. Then there was the matter of the rundown neighbourhood they lived in. The roads roared ceaselessly with traffic impossible to navigate. The pavements were a constant mess of broken bottles, of piss and puke and common foodstuffs that to canines could be like cyanide. Meanwhile in what passed for a local park unpredictable breeds of rottweilers and pitbulls and ridgebacks romped the sorry strip of vegetation, snarling and unmuzzled.

Frank felt the hazards were endless in the city. He hoped one day to have Angy trained to walk by his side unleashed. But that day was a long way off. He worried too that he was sabotaging some essential part of her nature in the city, keeping her inside so much and on such a short tether when they were out. Maybe he needed to be more patient, but there were times, staring in Angy's eyes, he thought he detected an emptiness there, that she might be depressed.

So the next time Frank had a few days off work he called his parents to tell them he would come down with the dog. His parents lived beside a forest in the countryside. They had only seen photos of Angy, and Frank hadn't been home since summer. At least there he would be able to let Angy run free for the first time, no leash, no harness, no nothing. If things went well, he might even begin going home more. It would be good for the dog, after all, the wide open spaces and the clear air of the heights.

Frank exited the southbound motorway and drove the last hour through the hills and finally up the driveway of his childhood home. His parents laughed out loud when he walked through the front door holding the dog in his arms like a newborn. He let Angy down on the kitchen floor. She was an instant hit with his parents, the way she wriggled her rear in sheer excitement when meeting new people, the look she gave you with her head bowed, something so beseeching in the eyes.

"So this is the Angy we've been hearing all about," his father said.

"That's right."

"There's breeding in her," his mother said, dipping her head down to the dog's.

Unusually, his parents didn't object to Angy jumping up on the furniture, and even agreed to letting her sleep inside. This was never the way pets were treated in this house when Frank was a boy.

"Ah she's a pure dote," his father said. "The city girl."

"It can be a bit of a warzone in the city with a dog."

"The small house, I suppose," his mother said.

"More so outdoors. I'm curious to see how she gets on here. All the freedom."

His mother and father exchanged a look and he was about to ask was there an issue, but just then a knock at the door interrupted.

It was his uncle.

"Hello, stranger," his uncle said and clapped him on the back with a hand. A bottle of the good whiskey was brought out.

"Her coat is soft as a rug," his uncle said as he petted Angy down.

"Oh, all the good living above," his father said.

His uncle explained how he'd run over his own dog with his car last week. He was gutted, he said.

"Here," his father said, addressing Frank, "tell the one about the time you brought the quare one down."

"What?"

"Remember, the quare one you brought down one Christmas."

"Oh," his mother said, "the vegetarian."

"With her olives," his father said. "Like pellets you'd poison a rat with."

He took a sip of his drink. They were referring to his college girlfriend, from years back. He remembered now. He'd arrived home with her for the holidays. She was an only child, had grown up with a string of much-loved labradors who'd been more like siblings than any kind of pet. "So we drive into the yard, I make the introductions. But I've a sense something is missing. I can't put my finger on it. Then it dawns on me. The dog! Dog's missing. Kojak, wasn't it?"

"A right fucker," his father said with emphasis.

"So I says, 'Where's Kojak?' and without missing a beat Daddy answers, 'Ah the auld bastard was pulling all the clothes off the line. So I took him up the woods and shot him.'"

His uncle was beside himself with laughter. He was convulsing in laughter. Everyone was laughing.

"So ... so I look over to my girlfriend. Now you should see the face on her. She's ... she's thinking this is *Deliverance* or something. With the banjos, right? I mean, her jaw *drops*."

"Hardly said a word the whole Christmas," said his father.

"Sat there reading her books," his mother said.

"But that dog was a right fucker," his father went on. "You'd go away, and when you came back the whole clothesline would be down on the ground and his Lordship has made a little *nest* for himself. *Under* the clothesline."

"We wouldn't be that cruel to you, would we, Angy?" his mother said. Angy had leapt into her lap.

"In fairness, I'd find it hard putting a bullet between her ears," his father said, refilling their glasses.

"You better not even think about it," his mother said. "She might be the closest I get to a grandchild."

"Sure I don't even have the gun anymore."

His parents' back garden was really more a field, an acre of shrubs, the remains of rockeries and vegetable patches gone wild. Angy loved it there when he let her out the next morning, disappearing between the pampas grass growing over the septic tank, digging up divots all over the flowerbeds, chasing after birds in the bushes. She sniffed at everything. Everything was new to her. Frank watched her, and he felt happy watching her. Angy was at last in her element, and his only regret was that they'd have to return to the city so soon.

He was coming round the side of the house with Angy when he saw a neighbour walking up the driveway. The neighbour must be in his late seventies now. He was looking a lot frailer since Frank had last seen him. Before they'd even said hello the neighbour asked would he breed pups off Angy.

"But she's only a pup herself."

"You'd fetch serious money for the bitches."

"I'm having her spayed."

"*Spayed!*" The neighbour was examining Angy's gums, her jaws pulled roughly apart. "She's pedigree, you're mad."

"A pity you've never been spayed," Frank felt like saying.

His father came out to the yard. "Well."

"Hey, have all the barbers gone on strike up there in the city," the neighbour said in a loud voice and jerked a thumb at Frank. It was true, he hadn't cut his hair in some time.

"Down, Angy," Frank said and she freed herself from the neighbour's grip.

"It's not a strike they're on at all," his father said. "If you ask me, they're all dead."

The neighbour began to laugh.

Frank took Angy over the road. He knew his father was only entertaining the neighbour. That neighbour had brutally beaten his boys when they were young. None of them spoke to him anymore. His father had told him all about the neighbour after one of the boys hanged himself, over in Australia.

Frank's homeplace was beside a forest, a commercial forest of planted pines that were in need of logging. All these mountainy hillsides had been taken over by the forestry commission. Nothing but marginal soils around here, there were monotonous pine plantations over all the heights now. At least something could thrive here, but he had never liked the pines. There was something dirty about them, something depressing, the sticky resin, the light all blocked out on the lifeless forest floor. One of his first recurring dreams involved this forest. In the dream he was always staring out his bedroom window, watching on as a fearsome band of Apache Indians strafed through the trees, on their way to murder him. He turned into the forest now, letting Angy off the leash. She sped over the rutted path, her gait like that of a miniature horse. Frank laughed. She looked back after a short dash, as if seeking permission.

"Go on," he ushered, "explore." He was always frozen to his bed in a paralyzing fear in the dream, even though somehow he always woke before the Apache raid reached the house.

The path rose steeply in sharp switchbacks. A short stretch on a burned-out car was buried in a culvert. The disused quarry you couldn't see anymore, it had been swallowed by gorse, by ferns, by a stand of some native hardwood. Often dead sheep were dumped in there when he was a child. He rounded the shoulder of the rise, fast-running streams roaring down the steep banks either side of the path.

He came out on a treeless ridge, high above the village at this vantage. He supposed visitors admired the view. The village was nestled in a crease near the bottom of a valley that fanned out in a sort of amphitheatre. There was the graveyard where his grandparents' plot was, the church and its bell tower hanging in the air, the national school he had attended, the two pubs bookending the single dreary street. A fine clear day,

DAVID RALPH

formations of wispy clouds scrolling across the sky. And a lot more houses around the village now. All these monster ranch-like residences with the ostentatious stone pillars out front, absurd names like *El Sur* embossed on big plaques affixed to intimidating wrought-iron gates. He didn't understand it, for so long he had never wanted any part in it. He shook his head. And rumours of a swingers' club in the village his sister had told him about one night they'd been drinking together and they both laughed in queasy revulsion.

He looked around. He'd almost forgotten the dog there. "*ANGY,*" he called. "*ANGY …*"

And there she was, her inquiring head poking out from round a bend. "Come here," he said, "good girl."

Nearing the crest of the hillside he could feel the strain in his calves. Several trees had been uprooted here, the victims of storms, their blackened twisted roots rearing out of the ground. Angy kept running up ahead, darting off in all directions, disappearing, circling back. This was good for her, her confidence. He couldn't patrol her every move forever. The spacing between the rows of tall pines all but vanished now, the forest floor covered in nothing but a carpet of mossy green scrub, only the smallest sprig of light. Wasn't there a mass rock up here somewhere? His teachers had told them about it, how the celebrants risked certain death if they were caught.

The plantation peaked sharply. All over the wasteground around the summit were spills of diesel oil, empty jerrycans, stacks of logs piled into pyramids. Frank and his friends used to climb log pyramids like these as children, running along the top as fast as they could. How something terrible had not befallen them he couldn't fathom now. All it would take was one log to give, and next thing you were entombed at the bottom of them.

"Angy."

A long moment passed.

"*ANGY.*"

An agitation went through the undergrowth, a scurry of some small-sized—

Angy came barging down a burrow in the bank.

She drank deep from a puddle as they descended, gave chase to a rabbit that got away. He'd hunted rabbits himself up here with his father, who'd tried teaching him to shoot. He'd got a right belt off the hip of the rifle once. It kicked up off his shoulder as he fired, and fractured his jaw. That was the end of him as a hunter.

About halfway down Angy stopped dead, eyes clapped on something among the trees. Slowly he came up behind her, hunkered down. He could feel her heart going, it was hammering. When his gaze located what hers was locked on, he just stayed squatting there, in sheer simple amazement.

"Well now, Angelica," he whispered into her ear. "I see what you see."

Bar the occasional creaking of a branch, a volley of wingbeats exploding in the air, there was perfect silence now. And in a dimly-lit channel between the lines of trees a young deer stood staring out at them. Probably not much older than Angy, his guess was she was only a fawn. The pelt a greyish brown. He had to pin Angy down, she was straining beneath his grip. The fawn continued watching them. The fawn was so precisely still, she was poised for flight. Frank daren't move. The stillness went on, expanding, deepening, gathering. Better to just look at it. But no, he had to reach into his pocket for his phone. He was about to press click on the camera when some stupid notification buzzed, and at that the fawn's front legs reared up, and it broke for the darkness.

The following morning when she was let out Angy ran straight down the driveway for the forest. She ignored Frank's roars to come back, he had to sprint after her. He grabbed her by the scruff and swore at her. Tractors bombed along these roads at all hours. He pulled her back from the road. He had a small piece of business to attend to a few fields over from his parents'. The previous evening as the light was going he had seen a faded For Sale sign leaning dangerously down into the road as he drove to the local shop. When he got back he checked the local auctioneer's listings online. It was as he expected. A roadside field belonging to a widow who lived in the village had been up on the site for a long time. Now he came over to the field. He righted the auctioneer's sign, noted the number to call. Then he climbed the rusting red gate into the long grass. Angy squeezed herself underneath the bottom bar after him. The field was well sheltered from the elements by the high hedgerows. Ten thousand it was up for. An ideal spot for a log cabin by the ditch there, a bed of decking out back that would open out like a balcony onto the sweep of fields running down to the road below. He laughed to himself. He could picture it alright, he could be like those Russians with his little dacha among the hills. A nice project to work on with his father when he retired next year, they hadn't done manual work together like that in a long time. He'd wait until dinner to tell his parents his plans.

Back outside the driveway to the house Angy started pulling on the lead again. She could see the forest, her nose was twitching in anticipation.

"Alright so," he conceded, "you win," but as he reached the forestry gate he turned abruptly back to the house. He needed a jacket, there was a chill in the air today. He tied Angy to the gate.

Coming into the porch he could hear his mother talking in the kitchen. He heard his name spoken and realised his mother was on the phone with someone. He held back to listen. From her tone he was sure it was her sister she was talking to.

"Oh we're nearly certain that's what he's planning … That's what his father thinks anyway … From the way he's been talking since he got here …" His mother laughed. "Ah now stop, it's not me who said that …" and she laughed again. "Sure did any of the women ever last long with him … Ah a bit spoiled, like he goes around carrying her in his arms as if it's a baby … But we'll be landed with her before long, mark my words. He's planting a seed on this visit."

As quiet as Frank could he slipped out of the porch again. The sky was banded in blues as he ascended the heights into the pines. He was in quiet shock. *Planting a seed* … Is that all his parents thought of him? *From the way he's been talking* … What were they on about? He called Angy to come back. She had disappeared round a corner. He broke into a jog and tried putting his mother's voice out of his head. Taking a corner he spotted Angy and something among the branches flickered past his periphery. He stopped up. There was nothing there.

His last girlfriend had left him, ending it had been very much against his wishes. But then the flicker again. And then he caught a glance of it, another greyish fawn springing over the forest floor, and Angy was sprinting up the bank and in among the trees after it. "*ANGY*, back here *NOW*." But she was gone.

He scrambled up the bank after her. She arrowed between burrows in the undergrowth of the sloping terrain. He hurdled over stumps, low-slung boughs, crunching twigs and shoots underfoot. There was a threshing sound behind him, and he turned sharply. Nothing. He stopped to catch his breath. Nothing but the soughing high above in the trees. Then the threshing was to his left, then his right, it was coming closer, and then he saw them, two, three, no four fawns rushing over the earth, now visible in flashes, now screened by branches and trunks. Then they were gone, plunging down a darkened tunnel. After a moment Angy reappeared, and he hitched the leash on her harness.

"As if you'd last long around here," he said into her ear.

Out on the path he noticed a turn-off he hadn't seen the day before. A rough track pitted in deep machine grooves skirted the perimeter of the plantation here. A short distance on a sign warned of the dangers of trees being felled, showing the outlines of a man's face with a wide open mouth, his right hand held up before him. Below the image the sign warned: parts of the forest may have prohibited access. He kept following the perimeter path.

Angy was behaving better, she trotted along beside him, no tug or pull on the leash. He let her off again. These childish hopes he always had that things would be different this time.

The light was tawny through the branches now, the pines had thinned at this elevation. Some had a big white *X* painted over their trunks like they'd been condemned for some infraction. Several times Angy veered off the path, fussing at something among the pines. Each time she was gone that bit longer, but each time she came back without him having to shout. She was his dog, and he would look after her. He kept climbing.

"*It's not me who said that*," he said involuntarily in a high-pitched voice imitating his mother and kicked out at a rock.

The report of a gun echoed across the valley all of a sudden. This report was followed by another. Angy accelerated up behind him, ears cocked to investigate the disturbance. Probably a marksman culling deer on another plantation, those gunshots.

He cut into the trees. Hooking up over this height, he reasoned, was a shortcut back out onto the path near the summit from yesterday. Him and Angy would head back to the city today. There was no point in hanging around, he'd only end up getting into a row with his parents. Stones, flattened slabs, were stitched into the slope here. Maybe this led to the mass rock, he thought suddenly. A secret stairs the pilgrims erected to their place of worship. Angy was out of sight already. He stayed climbing the flattened slabs.

There was a break in the trees up ahead, a sort of clearing, and he remembered now the drawings the teachers had them do on the blackboard. It was set in such a clearing, the mass rock, carved out of a big boulder, the altar hewed straight from the stone. Snow wouldn't gather there, it was said, there'd be a ring of untouched grass even when snow lay thickly drifted everywhere else, and if you rubbed the rock it offered a cure, sore throats, skin conditions, all manner of ailments.

From nowhere Angy came bulleting towards him. She crouched at his feet. She was cowering. "What's wrong, pet?" She wouldn't look at him. "What happened?" He tried pulling her along but she dug her paws down, reversing her body backwards. "Come on, Angy," he pleaded but she stayed pushing her body backwards.

The gun went off again across the valley, and at that a long bellowing noise went up among the nearby pines. Then there was the threshing through the trees again, only louder this time, much louder, and now branches were breaking, saplings snapping, it was as if the earth churned—

The stag launched itself at Frank before he could react, the impact from the animal's head slamming him to the ground. Then the stag sprung up on its hind legs, pucked him all over with its front hooves. But kicking out his own legs Frank managed to scooch backwards in under a fallen tree.

Now the stag attacked again, its antlers stabbing at the trunk. Frank felt like the trunk would split, the power behind the blows. Then the antlers snagged in the trunk momentarily; Frank made it to his feet and, in an adrenal rush, ran for his life. The pain coursing through his left side was excruciating, the stag must have punctured his flesh there. He pushed past more pines, and when he felt it was safe, he looked around. The stag was lost from view. The stag was gone. He spat soil from his mouth. He called Angy but no sounds formed. He tried calling again, more soil spilling from his mouth.

Angy was barking, more insistent than usual. The barks were coming from the clearing. His legs almost gave as he stumbled up the slope. He reached inside a pocket for his phone, but there was no reception. In the clearing grass grew over the ground in tussocky clumps, and there, right in the centre, stood the mass rock. He couldn't believe it. It was exactly as he'd sketched it all those years ago. Angy was pacing the altar. He stumbled once more. If he could only reach the mass rock, only a few paces more. Angy barked again, like she was calling to him. Her coat looked resplendent, an unreal sheen off it, and a heat was rising from her. A terrible lightness came over him. He held out a hand for balance but taking another step he clutched at his side—and now he was flat on his back. He summoned every shred of his strength but it was like his whole ribcage had caved in. He lay helpless on the frigid earth. Angy stretched out across the altar. She licked at the rock with her tongue. She cut him a look and he noticed her markings … the markings on her face had changed, Frank was sure of it, the borders had shifted, been redrawn. One more time he tried to drag himself upright, he strained every sinew, every muscle. Futile.

In the air the branches of the desolate pines encircling him were sweeping over and back. They sounded more like the sea, like small waves lapping. He recalled now something about the high ground, something about the rutting season, someone from long ago warning him to be careful over the high ground at the end of the rutting season. His body grew cold. His breathing laboured. But he hadn't really been listening to whoever it was warning him. A deep tiredness was seeping into him. He coughed up more soil. His eyes closed.

Then the village church bells rang out across the valley. Soon it would be dark and the stars would come out, one by one, and the Apaches were

　　　　　　　　　　　　　　　　　　　　　　DAVID RALPH

very close now, they were closing in on him, the Apaches had never been so close. The most fearsome Apache had a tomahawk, a feral slash of warpaint down his cheeks. He could feel the nearness of the Apache's powerful muscled body, no dream had ever been so convincing, and in a violent manoeuvre that was shocking in its swiftness the sharpened edge of the Apache's tomahawk sliced brutally across his throat. Blood was pooling all around him, spurting from him in hot jets. He felt for the first time that he might not wake from this dream, that this dream might be all there would be forever. But sinking down deeper into the horror of the dream he told himself that, like always, like ever since the days he was that frightened little boy lying frozen in his bed, he would of course wake on time, and the dream would stop.

Robert René Galván

Banyan

Lord Krishna said … the banyan tree with roots
above and branches below is imperishable; the
Vedic scriptures are the leaves of that tree …
– Bhagavad Gita 15:1

It sang for 150 years
beneath the cruel
sun, a Vedic hymn
vaulted from
wandering roots into
a cathedral of
shadows,
from its vantage
above the village
witnessed the
burning of paradise,
itself
kindling into
the night,
spirits fled
with smoke;
by morning a decimation,
a wailing of
unfathomable loss,
airships stranded,
no escape
but into the sea.

Stationary, bereft of
leaves, it towers above the
ruins like an abandoned
temple where the blue god
rests in an arch,
beckons migrant
spirits return to
smoldering trunks,
a locus
like the bird of yore*.

My father, Roberto Arispe Galván, references the Phoenix as "the bird of yore" in his poem 'Cycles.'

Hannah Linden

Mist

I remember the first time I saw the moor through his eyes.
I had been crying at the wisps which kept moving along
over the grass as he said *ahh will you look at that*
and sighed in that way of letting go of everything—
lifted his face into the drizzle and let the rain
run down his collar for the thrill.

A sheep wandered by and he dropped to his knees, took my hand
to show me how to pet her, in that slow patient way of his,
not allowing me to pull away from the grease of it. He knew
I was too cold to enjoy this, too afraid of everything,
too ready to apologise. He wanted me to be bold, at least then,
when he could still bear it, before there'd be no more time

to explain why you should be who you had to be
before the mist gets inside you and blurs the edges.

Hannah Linden

Dear Kafka

We are saddened to be associated forever with your name. We know you didn't specify but you should have known what people are with their addiction to pins and down.

Sir, we are not dirty. Or depressed even. And we, of course, think we are beautiful. After my daughter read your book, Sir, she cried. *Think what happened in Europe afterwards, Papa.*

I tell her we cannot hold you responsible for that. But it is hard to reassure the young who sometimes don't understand their elders' intentions.

But it's happening again, Papa: look at the election results. Look at the rise of the right. They will push more people into their bedrooms and they'll never get out again, Papa.

Even the young have to harden themselves. So many of us, Kafka. So many of us in the cracks and dark places under the couch. And the clerks don't come to check on us in person any more. Even the scraps they throw us are getting scarce.

Anastasia Jill

Coughing Fish

Russell picks his teeth with a piece of bass spine, removing a hunk of meat stuck in his molars. He is a man of routine, my brother, eating fish three meals a day; shrimp and grits for breakfast, pan-fried bass for lunch. For dinner, he eats salmon – plain salmon with coleslaw. He saves the bones of every dish, placing them on the kitchen counter.

"They have a use," my brother tells me. "Every part of the fish has a use."

I tease him every time. It's easy to tease my brother when he's so serious about a topic so punitive. "Our family has lived off the rez for a couple hundred years. We don't need to save the throwaway parts of an animal," I say.

The joke lingers in the air, a stink worse than the fish. My brother doesn't throw away anything. He's what his doctor would call a hoarder. That's the way it's been since we inherited the house last year. Russell and I handled the death of our mother in different ways; I started smoking two packs of cigarettes a day. He saved everything that came in proximity to the house. Our cats eat and sleep where they shit, we have no path from the living room to the bed. There are big plastic jugs of mystery brown liquid in my brother's bathroom. I haven't asked him about it. I have no desire to know exactly how much he saves.

The only room in the house left untouched is the kitchen, save for the fishbones and odd piles of year-old mail. Russell spends most of his time here, cooking meals, paying bills, watching television. Today, like each weekday, I get home around four after my shift at the pharmacy. He ate a late lunch, he says, but is already thinking of dinner.

"I think we're out of salmon," he says.

"Can't be," I say. "You just went to the store the other day."

"No, we're out, I'm sure of it." Not once does he consult the fridge. "What are you doing this afternoon?"

"Foraging for the mattress in my room."

He doesn't find the joke humorous. He is too busy worrying about fish, the bone from his lunch rolling like rice paper under his tongue.

"We need to go to the market. You're coming with me. I don't want to go alone."

I implore him to wait an hour, maybe two. "I've been on my feet all morning. I really just want to take a nap."

The blacks of his eyes start flying like vigorous polyps against a water-shot screen. My brother doesn't like uncertainty, panics at the slight of routine disturbance. "What if the market runs out of salmon?"

"They won't."

"It's a popular dish during Lent."

"It's the middle of September. I think you're fine."

He looks at me, nervous, like the world will end if he doesn't have fish. He's closer to thirty than twenty, and five years my senior, but looks to me to cater to him, as mother often did. I don't respond. I turn and say, "I need a cigarette."

It takes me a while to get out of our garage with its three cars and refrigerators. When I'm outside, I don't even care that there's only one cigarette left in my pack. I light it up and inhale, my guppy lips hoping cancer comes to me swiftly as it did Mom. Our mother never smoked or drank a day in her life, but still dropped dead at fifty-five, leaving me to take care of my brother. The doctors said her death had natural causes, but I think it was stress. Oh, boy, do I *bet* it was stress. A few months of my brother makes my own heart constrict. He sucks up oxygen with his neurotic little gills.

He will kill me. Or someday, I'll kill him.

A few minutes pass, the long cigarette shrinks to the size of a thumb. I suck in the smoke until it hurts me to cough. I throw it on the pile and go back to the kitchen. Russell has broken the fish bone and added it to his own pile. I don't want to wait until he has a panic attack.

"Alright, get your wallet," I say to him. "Let's go and get you some fish."

We have one working car left – a 1970s Volvo that smells of ammonia and has a layer of slime on the unused back seats. It eats gas and moves slow, but can get us to Saigon Market. I refuse to let Russell drive, though I am falling asleep at the wheel. He keeps me awake with his incessant questioning.

"One more time. What if they're out of salmon?"

"They won't be."

"But if they are?"

"I don't know. Get a fucking crab or something."

He is silent after that.

"What's the big deal?" I say.

"Mom and I had salmon every night."

"Mom hated fish."

"Well, she made it for me."

I tell him to be quiet. I need to focus on the road, what with the sun frothing light across the windshield. When I do speak, it's a reminder, "I don't get paid until the end of the week so let's keep this cheap." And he promises to do just that. "Good," I say. "I need to get some cigarettes on the way home."

Twenty minutes later, we arrive at the market, Russell running out before the car is in park. I join him inside, finding him in the back with his nose pressed to the fish cooler like a child looking in a candy store. This serves no purpose; he selects the same thing every time. Salmon, always salmon, more salmon than one person could possibly eat. I crouch to his side. This particular carcass gasps under the glass, cold steam clouding the reflection.

"They look like they're coughing," Russell says.

"Fish don't cough."

"They do when they're dying, when they're on land, I suppose."

A man comes up in an apron. "What can I get for you today?"

Russell points at the salmon, asking for four or five pounds. The man slices the fish, wrapping the fillets in slick, waxy paper. He weighs and totals it, sticking the price tag on the top. He hands it over the counter, but I note an error.

"Excuse me," I say. "The sign says salmon is ten dollars a pound."

"That was yesterday. Today it's twelve."

I scoff. "That's bullshit."

The man shrugs. "That's business."

Russell grabs my shoulder and whines, and I don't know what for. He'd be a pain in the ass to deal with sans his salmon. I take the package and

ANASTASIA JILL

stomp to the register, where I throw it in front of the cashier, who rings me up. The purchase takes the last of my twenties, leaving me with a single and some coins. I grab the plastic bag and throw it at my brother.

In the car, he says, "Thank you."

"Yeah, right." I veer the car into traffic without looking.

We pass red lights and traffic, cover a few blocks before Russell asks, "What about your cigarettes?"

I say, "We can't afford them now."

"I'm sorry."

"Sure you are."

"Veronica?"

"What?" I snap.

He keeps his head down and says, "Nothing." And we say nothing else to each other for the short ride home. Once the car is in park, Russell dashes for the kitchen. When I enter the house, he's feeding the cats juice from the bottom of a tuna can.

I do not speak to him as I take off my sweater and throw down my purse. With nothing to calm me and nowhere to go without climbing stacks of garbage, I knock the stacks of envelopes from my place at the table. I watch him be tender with the cats, then add the empty tuna can to the living room mess. Once he is done, he faces me, trembling.

"Go on," I say. "Make the salmon. You had to have it so damn bad."

Like our mother, I don't like fish, but am out of patience to cook my own dinner tonight. Russell puts two fillets on the stove and asks me to get the olive oil from the fridge. I open the door – also a rancid mess – and after pushing aside empty cartons of milk I find – in white wrapping – the salmon we purchased the other day.

I stare at it for a moment. Exhale once, then twice. "Russell, come here."

He lowers the burner then faces me.

I point to the package shoved to the back of the fridge.

His voice lacks apologetics as he says, "Oh, oops."

"*Oops*," I echo. "All you have to say is *oops*?"

His eyes tremble to the point of tears, and I know I am not as calm as I trick myself into thinking. He's backing away, hands pushing against the stream of my temper. "Veronica, I'm sorry. I forgot. I'm really sorry, I forgot." He doesn't get a chance to finish his thoughts before I grab him by the shoulders and shove him into the wall. This isn't hard. I'm six inches taller and have fifty pounds on him. Plus, he is too scared to try to fight me once I roar, "*I am so sick of your bullshit Russell!*"

I grip him so tight that his collarbone bunches up to his throat. He cannot breathe, and I can keep it that way. I could end this right now, leave him limp as a dirty sweater and add him to the pile. The cats could sleep on his thighs and chest.

I drop him the instant the thought grabs me. I couldn't do that to my brother.

Once I let him go, he's coughing, arms flopping like fish on a boardwalk. The salmon is burning on the skillet behind him, steam colliding with the chill of the fridge.

"I'm sorry," I tell him. "I am so sorry."

He grabs my shoulder to steady himself. His touch is gentle, and his words are punctuated by whooping coughs. "It's okay, Veronica. It's okay."

I take him by the hand and place him at the table. The cats crowd around his feet, though he has no food to offer this time. Tossing the burned fish in the trash, I take the fresh pack from the fridge, frying it with olive oil and capers, serving it with a side of coleslaw. I sit across from him as he eats.

"What about you?" he asks.

What about me? I remind him, "I don't like fish."

Once he is done, I take his plate and set it in the sink. I turn the faucet on, the remains sliding down the moldy drain. I leave the water on hot, trying to remove more sludge from the hole. Smoke rises and burns the leftovers until every part of the sink is purged.

I turn to the bone pile, and think of discarding that trash too. Instead, I pick a bone and smush it between my molars, crunching hard at each end. Once it is small, I push it between my teeth, suck deep, and exhale.

Christine Barkley

(Oil on Seawater, Transferred to Canvas)

I imagine she lives a year
hauled away and daily
paints the bay, knows it
at once too cold to swim
or stay. Out of frame
to her a man has been
hitched, and raises
his dominant hand,
and does not always do,
I hope, what has been
threatened. Of course he does
mean to make an island
of her. Of course she uses
brush instead of knife,
holds with her right.
She will not remember
which sea, what stroke,
whose hands. Why
of shades she leans
to the blues of green.
If our eyes, I wonder.
Or how he returns her or
with her to the landlock
of new world harbors,
and children to anchor,
and a chill to bear. Still I dream
from the village she could see
the river, some strait to turn
swells to oil if still she had
wishes. Or the will

to learn use of the other
hand, or of breath
to float. From her
and to shore descending
I let swirl the silt
in each hand. What is left
a submission to common
gulls, native of any
ocean. And the right,
if ever claimed, is odd
as an easel moored
to breakwater, and artist
unknown.

CHRISTINE BARKLEY

Christine Barkley

Imprints

Pink from bent light, the skin
of his nose has now flayed.
I alone become comfortable
in this routine of lashing
down the hours
of the day,
which will keep me alive
and quiet as long as
I like. Some things occur
as a result of hands
and of mouths,
and by movement
through a field
of fields. I can't say
what I have done but I will say
something has happened.

Today he is worried,
loudly. Today I attend
to the day. Today
another sheep goes
missing, no one to blame
but unfixed locks and black
holes. Some things quiet stay
quiet for fear of being held
accountable. I can't say.

Today a new post
is anchored, a wire
grounded according
to good practice.
Instructions are followed
always, dangers signed
when possible. Some things occur
impossibly. Some things occur
when I move too slowly,
freeze, fawn. I can't say
what has happened
though I know
what can be done.

What is done
is done. I can't say
the sheep have gone
missing. I can see
signs of movement
through the fields
of field, and of
mouths. In the flocking
darkness he rises before
touching the sunburn
with his tongue,
barks once to say
something is happening.

CHRISTINE BARKLEY

David Mullin

Ornithomancy

I took pains to determine the flight of crook-taloned birds, marking
which were of the right by nature, and which were of the left, and
what were their ways of living, each after his kind.
    – Aeschylus, *Prometheus Bound*

Face north: begin the inauguration.

"A ...-bird came in flying ... / It came in flying ..."
"(n number of) ...-birds came in flying .../ They came in flying ..."

From which directions do the birds come?
(from the favourable area in the direction of the unfavourable area)
To where do they fly?
(from the unfavourable area in the direction of the favourable area)

How do they fly?
(it goes on flying while turning back)
Do they fly against the wind?
(it does not make a turning back in the flight)

From what quarter do they bring the weather?
(the first and third quadrants, the second and fourth quadrants)

Which species are by nature favourable and which sinister?
(owl, crow, raven)
are they *(birds of wing)* or *(birds of crying)*?

(They came in flying back from the favourable [area]
upwards, and flew away in front.)

And what auguries from
the unpredictable bird
that claw-tangles your hair,
the black bird that nests in
St Kevin's outstretched palm,
the bones
and black feathers
on the reservoir shore?

And from these who by degrees
fail to return in the spring,
or the long-necked birds
that arrive undocumented
too early in the autumn?

"A ...-bird flew away ... / It flew away ..."
"n (number of) ...-birds flew away ... / They flew away ..."

*Phrases in italics taken from Hittite bird oracle texts of c.1350-1190 BCE
which appear in Yasuhiko Sakuma (2013), 'Terms of Ornithomancy in
Hittite',* Tokyo University Linguistic Papers (TULIP) *33, 219-238.*

DAVID MULLIN

Louise Kim

urban sonnet

another poem published with a spelling error—
not mine—and i wrestle with the fact that
possession and responsibility are not mine
to possess. in thought, i almost run into a flower
stand. didn't mrs. dalloway say she would get the flowers
herself? or something like that. in thought,
i look beyond the sidewalk i look below the moon.
police van double parked, two lovers leaving
the strand. i hope that when i speak with you,
i get my message across. your face haunts me as i walk
the streets, meandering right into a puddle.
the water feels cool seeping through my shoes.
perhaps, i will never learn to be content
with my own permeability. perhaps, i will never learn.

Diarmuid Cawley

Adults

On rare hot days
as children, we'd discover
worlds. And everything new,
wondrous, and terrifying stretched
without time. In full growth
the day with all its light resisting—

marching against oppression,
building dams on streams, creating
new flow, signing pacts in blood,
forming our language in secret.
Now and then we'd learn about death,
a stationary animal, its bones drying

in the sun, fascinating maggots feasting,
the matted fur rippling when poked
with a stick. Decay became soil
upon which we built statehood,
keeping the crowd from the other street out.
When their backs were turned

we'd raid and ransack their huts,
smashing down doors, burning magazines,
pen-knifing footballs, we the lords
and them only flies; they'd retaliate
when their time came.
Our lives reflected in the smashed glass

of abandoned factories, crumbling
regimes camouflaged in suburbia,
where ambition knew no bounds,
until unseen voices ran us off,
covered in scratches, tattooed
in mud, holding stitched sides.

Diarmuid Cawley

Washed

We washed a bag of apricots at a roadside tap.
Swollen hands refreshed of grime, you fed them
to me as we drove all day, into the dark
from Fez to Marrakesh, my arm red
from August, two open windows drawing hot winds
over us, every pore dust-filled and dry.
How tenderly you tore the fruit, removing each stone,
halves of ripe yellow flesh by the edge of the desert
where we did not feel welcome.
In a carpeted room with low lights and wood—
after we had showered, after we had eaten,
after we had searched dim narrow streets
—we got to know each other better.

Brendan Mac Evilly

Being and Swimmingness

ONE
1 February

I wake in the middle of the night for the toilet, look at the phone, 3.30 a.m., another two and a half hours of sleep that never come. I lie awake and turn over forty or fifty times in anticipation of February's first swim, finally rolling out at 5.45 a.m. I'm in the car by 5.58 a.m. with a flask of tea.

Driving in the dark along the canal from Rialto, the swans are still tucked into their bed of wings. At 6.04 a.m. the Sea Area Forecast comes on the radio. Mace Head Automatic, Roches Point Automatic, Buoy M1, Buoy M2. It's lonesome to think of those meteorological blobs, bobbing away in the cold, all morning, all day, all night. The presenter reads the forecast so slowly I find my mind wandering, missing sea temperatures, wave heights. It is the most boring and the most reassuring news piece of the day. The wind still blows, the sea still rises and falls, the sky precipitates in varying qualities and quantities.

Getting out of the car, there is only the sound of early-risen birds and the hush-suck-hush of sea on Sandycove Beach. The tide is fully out.

TWO

"I think therefore I am" – a line of thinking that injected a wave of paranoia into the study of philosophy for centuries to come. René Descartes had some serious doubts about the objects of everyday experience – do they exist in the real, material world or do they only exist as objects of consciousness, as phantoms of our mind? It led to an acutely tiresome conversation that distracted philosophers from the more interesting questions of philosophy: what is it to exist as a human being? What is it to live well?

Edmund Husserl, born in 1859, two hundred and sixty-three years after Descartes, found a convenient way to bypass the problem. Who cares whether or not all these things in front of us are real? One way or another, we perceive them. We needn't call them 'objects' when 'objects of consciousness' will do. Do these objects of consciousness correlate to things with a concrete existence outside our minds? It doesn't matter. What matters is the visual, aural, oral, olfactory experiences of our daily lives and the psychological states of fear, anxiety, joy that go with them.

Husserl wanted to drop the question of external existence and begin a discussion about the experiences themselves. Not just experiences of physical objects, but of situations, sensations, states of mind. Let's analyse how we interact with these objects of consciousness rather than worrying about whether they correlate with an objective reality. Let's observe the flow of consciousness. Husserl called it phenomenology – the rigorous recording of existence as it happens, describing the world as it appears and unfolds.

By applying the phenomenological approach – a methodology rather than a set of theories – Husserl believed the observing mind could peel away learned wisdom, clichés, and preconceived notions to get at the thing in itself, thus creating more accurate descriptions of our lived reality. Phenomenology would help us to question received ideas and routines. It could scrape away the filters of ideology – fascism, Marxism, capitalism, religion – that obscure our view.

It could also tell us something essential about humanity. By observing how the mind observes, by recording how the mind records, we could generate new understandings of our psychological states, of how we fear, love, desire. Husserl's was a bold move away from the science of things toward the significance of things.

This ability to extract meaning from bare, unadulterated existence became hugely popular among philosophers, psychologists, novelists, artists and thinkers of all kinds over the following century. Practices and conclusions of phenomenology influenced a whole movement of philosophy – existentialism – that concerned itself with individuals and their personal existence, freedom, anxiety and authenticity.

In October 2016, a slowly forming plan became a commitment – to swim in the sea each day through the month of February, when sea temperatures are at their lowest; and where possible, to do this before first light. I had been swimming, or to be more precise, floating, with increasing regularity over the past three years. I had a growing sense that floating in cold water gave birth to a very peculiar sense of existence, though I couldn't put my finger on it. Nor could I figure out if I had committed myself to the project out of self-love or self-loathing. Was this about an authentic desire to swim in the sea or did I want to create an image of myself as a hardy sea soul? Over twenty-eight days, I attempted to deploy the phenomenological approach to see what results it might yield.

Husserl said, "Give me a cup of coffee and I will make phenomenology out of it." The body of liquid I hoped to describe was certainly grander. But I wanted to approach it as Husserl suggested, avoiding clichés, habits of thought, distractions. Describing not just the object but the lived experience of it.

THREE
1 February continued

Around the corner at the Forty Foot, three or four people have gathered for the daily 6.30 a.m. meet. They talk by a battery-powered lamp hung from the coat hanger of the concrete shelter. After a minute of undressing, another swimmer emerges silently from the sea. It's still too dark to see faces. Too dark to see the water all around.

I step down to the sea, trying to pick out the white of my feet as I walk, not wanting to slip on the concrete that has been poured into this granite crevice. Rock that was once quarried from this area to build the Martello tower looming behind.

At the last carved stone step, my toes search for the edge. Are they waiting above to hear my splash, I wonder. With the tide so low, the staircase to the sea has grown longer and I am out of sight. I dash water over my face and torso. I take stock of myself, look back over my shoulder. Stars fill the still-black sky.

I leap forward, head-first. First is the shock of cold, then I open my eyes. The sea is an opaque version of the sky above, a milk-stout black.

The sense of elation is immediate and uncomplicated. At this level of silence, the only sound is my heavy breathing – the body's response to such cold. My eyes pick out what little acts of light there are: flashes from distant islands and edges – The Baily, Kish Bank, the Muglins – and the stars overhead. I lie on my back and float.

When you eat ice-cream or drink a cold drink, the sudden temperature drop in your mouth causes blood vessels to constrict. The body reacts quickly by dilating the same vessels to increase blood flow and reheat the area. The rapid constriction–dilation response triggers pain receptors which the brain interprets as a headache. With my head submerged under water, something similar is happening, though this particular brain-freeze is externally sourced and lacking the sugar to sweeten the deal.

I swim in to shore but, wanting to hold the moment, turn around to swim out again until the cold starts to bite my feet.

As the others dry up and leave, taking the lamp, another person arrives:

"Who's that?" she calls to the silhouette I make for her.

"A newcomer," I say.

"Oh," she says, and pauses. "How do you know you're a newcomer?"

It seems an odd question. And far too metaphysical for this early hour.

"Well I know I haven't swam in the dark before," I tell her.

It's not till I'm driving home that I remember this is untrue. Memories come back of Ventry at the age of seventeen, three young men skinny-dipping on the beach, around 1.00 a.m. The others too sober or sensible to swim at night have stolen back to the house with our shoes and clothes, leaving only two towels and one pair of shoes between three of us. We navigate the short but painful stone-chip road, at times taking jockey backs from the person wearing the shoes, or hopping on one foot when it's our turn to wear one.

Another time in Montauk, after the nightclub has closed, we swim in the nearby lake, finding out later that it's inhabited by snapping turtles.

Another time again, on New Year's Eve, coming from a house party by the Portobello Bridge, crossing the road in my boxers to dive into the canal at 2.00 a.m., then back to the party for a shower and tea and drink, none of which warms me.

BRENDAN MAC EVILLY

"What's your name again," the lady asks me as she leaves, still in darkness.
"Brendan," I say.
"I'm Liz." She says, "Not that we'll recognize each other the next time we meet."

FOUR

As well as inventing the phenomenological approach, Husserl developed the notion of intentionality, the way our mind appears always to be directed at things, to reach out and grab hold of things in the world. If I'm hammering a nail, for example, the mind appears to be directed towards the hammer, the nail, the act of hammering. My consciousness in some kind of communion with them.

One of Husserl's many students and followers, Martin Heidegger, took these ideas further by bringing our minds even closer to the objects. He coined the term *dasein* – 'being in the world' or literally 'being there', to describe the peculiar kind of beings that we are – embodied entities, thrown into the world, who cope skilfully in given social and cultural contexts. Hyper aware of our immediate surroundings, but aware also of our existence in a wider universe, aware and anxious about our mortality and our personhood. A woman hammering a nail does not continually focus on the hammer hitting the nail, says Heidegger. A man driving a car does not continually think "I am driving, I'm driving, keep driving." Far from being focused on what we're doing, as Husserl had described, we can at the very same time be deeply engaged in political discussion or sexual fantasy, or anxiously awaiting some event which may never occur.

It's only when things go wrong, Heidegger pointed out – when the hammer misses the nail or when the car veers off-centre and thum-thum-thums over the cat's eyes – that we even remember we are hammering or driving, so busy is our mind with other activity, surrounded and engaging with a multiplicity of objects of consciousness.

Heidegger noticed how things appear as mattering to us, as being important in some way. He noticed too that we are always articulating, engaged in communication of one form or another in a wider context of significance. And perhaps most insightfully, he observed how *dasein* is always pressing into the future. Hammering or driving or worrying. I'm always doing something towards some explicit or implicit goal. Awareness of our future, of time itself, determines who we are as humans. Knowledge of an impending future determines our concern for one object, activity or person over another. Hence, the name of his greatest and most expansive thesis – *Being and Time*.

We are thrown into the world, says Heidegger, and are then conditioned by our family and friends, place, customs, the consequences of our genetics. But he shows how people can push beyond these learned, found-in situations. We're influenced by social norms, but still able to think and act beyond them.

Our efforts to step outside our normal modes of behaviour can cause a kind of existential anxiety. As we become increasingly aware of the infinite possibilities for every next action (or inaction), some people choose to reject or disown these possibilities. They prefer to accept the status quo – about the world out there but also about themselves. Disowning *dasein*, believes Heidegger, is an act of inauthenticity. But by accepting this truth about our being, the contingency of it, we're able to formulate new ways of being for ourselves; we are catapulted into a more authentic existence.

There are other consequences to this new awareness. We don't embrace projects with the conviction that we'll get some deep, final meaning from them; we don't believe the completion of our goals will help to make sense of our lives. But we don't drop all our projects because they fail to have meaning either. Responding to each unique situation with a clear and honest outlook makes us flexible, alive, or, as Heidegger said, "freu" – gay. Thus Heidegger's philosophy is one of individual, existential liberation and authentic living.

FIVE
6 February

Monday morning. Up at 6.00 a.m., in the car at 6.17. Pick up Aoife at 6.39. Arrive at the Forty Foot just before 7.00 a.m. A little windy but the water is calm, tide just breaching the lip of the concrete where we jump off. The water is no colder than usual but there is a great pleasure from giving voice to *eeps* or *yelps* or *burrs* of bodily exhilaration on coming up for air.

"Good morning" shouts Aoife as she emerges from her dive. We have spent fifteen minutes together with muted commuter chatter, and more of the same quiet talk as we undress, but she is right, Good morning! Immersion in this shocking cold water is a second waking.

Aoife is a stronger swimmer than me. Or, Aoife is a swimmer, whereas I am mainly a sea-lounger. She swims to the first buoy whereas I paddle out just far enough for a view; Dublin Bay to the north and Dalkey Island to the south. In the south-east, the sky brightens. Pale pink and orange streaks appear between lines of cloud on the horizon. A cloudbank hanging over Ireland, a cloudbank hanging over Wales. The clearer space between where the light flares through is speckled with tiny puffs of cloud, like cannon balls burst in the air.

All focus is on the immediate moment, or the moment just to come. The next second, then the next, then the next. Attention must be paid just to keep afloat. Watching your position, making sure not to drift. Paying attention to body heat. And, for a moment, lying on your back to float in earnest.

This time, I even remember to think about what it is I'm thinking about, to observe myself observing. But it interferes with the natural flow of thoughts. I start to think about how I will record this in my diary, and how I can't write this for fear it proves points that are counter to my theory – that you cannot, in February-cold sea water, think beyond the present moment; that the insistence of the present moment for every millisecond of your attention distracts from the troubles of life. So I start to refocus on the freezing pang in my shins, the burning cold on the soles of my feet that increases in ferocity. Then I plunge my head beneath the water again, turning one last time towards the horizon to watch the sea fold in to shore.

On exit, another gent passes me on the steps. His black Labrador waits patiently by his clothes under the white-painted concrete shelter. He reaches down for handfuls of water, which he rubs over his body to acclimatize. The moment his body hits the water, the dog lets out a loud, extended whinny that continues as her friend disappears below the water and swims out into the low-lit morning.

"Your dog loves you," I tell him when he returns to dry land.

"Oh, she was crying again?" He smiles.

A moment later he turns to me. "Your friend has gone for a longer swim?"

There's a note of worry in his voice. Most swimmers, or most early-morning winter swimmers, would be back by now. Aoife is unusual in her ability, and desire, to swim for as long as she does. What this man is really saying to me is "Pay attention, you idiot. Don't you realize your friend is probably drowning?"

SIX

Jean-Paul Sartre had a chance to acquaint himself with Heidegger's *Being and Time* as a prisoner of war in Stalag 12D near the Luxembourg border. It was around this time that he was inspired to write his own mammoth work, *Being and Nothingness*. But it's in his slim and eminently readable volume *Existentialism and Humanism* that his ideas and those of the existentialist movement are best distilled, where he focuses on freedom and authenticity; where he shouts his existential clarion call: "existence before essence." That is to say, first we exist, then we decide who we are – through our beliefs, our choices, our projects.

For Sartre, no matter how restrictive our circumstances, no matter the extent to which our social and cultural contexts have dictated our life choices till now, we are always confronted with the present moment and the possibilities each moment gives us to choose anew, to invent new selves, directions, purposes.

"Thus, there is no human nature," says Sartre. "Man is nothing else but that which he makes of himself." *Existentialism and Humanism* is filled with similarly stark aphorisms:

"To choose between this or that is at the same time to affirm the value of that which is chosen."

BRENDAN MAC EVILLY

"Man is nothing else but that which he purposes; he exists only in so far as he realises himself, he is therefore nothing else but the sum of his actions, nothing else but what his life is."

"Life is nothing until it is lived."

Sartre recognised the consequences of such statements: "No doubt, this thought may seem comfortless to one who has not made a success of his life. On the other hand it puts everyone in a position to understand that reality alone is reliable; that dreams, expectations and hopes serve to define a man only as deceptive dreams, abortive hopes, expectations unfulfilled."

This raises questions for me about the kind of person that chooses for their project to float in cold sea water in the dark. Is mine an authentic response to the ultimate meaninglessness of any action, embracing the gaiety that comes from marking the sheer oddity and beauty of existence? Or should I feel anxious, guilty even, as often I do at my quietude in the face of national and global forces? Aren't there greater issues I might individually or collectively attempt to address with my leisure time?

Sartre, living through war, engaged in ideological battles between capitalism and communism, certainly lived up to his own words – confronting his own power to make individual choices that would determine the outcomes of cultural revolutions, putting most of our daily projects and dilemmas to shame.

But he recognised that inaction was a form of action too. That less dramatic choices could be value-decisions nonetheless, best illustrated by the story Sartre tells of a student who turns to him for advice. The student's brother was killed during the 1940 German offensive. He considers joining the Free French Alliance to avenge his brother, but is weighed down by responsibility to his mother whom he takes care of. She has already lost a child; she lives only for him. Torn between conflicting obligations, he must choose between acting on a personal or national stage. One choice offers action and meaning with a broader significance, but uncertain efficacy; the other fulfils an obligation of duty and love that will more certainly save the heart of one.

SEVEN
14 February

Seapoint today. I stopped here yesterday but a seasoned swimmer had just come from the water with a bloodied knee and a sore back. He warned me against swimming, so I went to Dún Laoghaire. Today at Seapoint it is calmer, but still swelly – orange weather warnings. As I creep into the water along the blue railing I'm forced back against it by the sea. I plant both feet into the concrete before each impending wave. But once I'm away from the iron-work and out to sea it feels safer, just like riding the waves of a western shore beach. The sole focus of my attention for the next few minutes is a lone gull bobbing on the water fifteen feet from my head. I swim towards it, but though it doesn't appear to move, it maintains its distance.

I play against the steely green waves that rise towards a grey sky. I look back now and then to check my distance from shore, and take pictures of the gull over and over with a waterproof camera. I've chased seals in this way too. They also keep their distance. Dipping up and down, reappearing, observing. What do they do in the sea all day? It seems such a long time to stay in one place. Do they know every inch of shoreline? Do animals ever go on holidays, travel? My gull may migrate, but does it ever fly anywhere unpredictable? Does it have notions, flights of fancy? Does a mood ever take it? Does it ever wonder?

I get out and dry. A woman of maybe sixty arrives. Just herself and myself, half naked by the shore on Valentine's Day. Her face is familiar from swims gone by. She swims daily but hasn't been in since last Thursday because of the weather. We have something new to talk about – the sea as ever, but a different aspect. Is it safe or not?

"I'm glad you're here," she says, "If there's nobody else around, you might get to thinking you're mad."

It's true, seeing another swimmer is reassuring. And you always hope they know the spot a little better than you do. We discuss yesterday's dangerous seas, today's tactics for entry, the safest approaches. I tell her she'll be fine. But as we're talking, the sea flexes, the tide washes in

BRENDAN MAC EVILLY

a little closer. I keep an eye. I have my towel wrapped round my togs, my jumper on.

Just as she reaches the blue railings, a wave comes in and sweeps her onto her back, drags her along the granite gangway for a couple of meters towards the overspill, towards the jagged rocks. And then the waves retreat, dragging her the other way, back out to sea.

It happens in a matter of a second and a half. And as I step forward, I'm aware how alike this is to keeping a bead on a plane in the sky, imagining it start to descend at a deathly angle or instantly explode in front of you. But this time the plane does explode, this time the worst thing is happening. Yet very quickly she has righted herself and the sea has all but disappeared. She watches it retreat, stares motionlessly, in anger or shock. I can see that she is considering going back in, to prove to herself that the sea is safe. But then she turns back, walks towards me, embarrassed by her fall. I feel guilty. I made her feel it was safe.

We try to explain it to each other, the fall. She tells me that it is best not to hold on to the bar, always to go with the flow of the sea, not to fight. She is trying to regain control of those few seconds of being at the sea's mercy. "It's really picked up in the last few minutes," I say. "It should be calming rather than strengthening as it reaches high tide." I imagine her head hitting a rock, or her body drifting out with the freak wave. I apologise to her.

Three more women arrive as I leave. The fallen lady is still there. She will tell her story again to those three women to talk herself out of shock. She will tell it again later that day, and on a number of occasions after. She will explain it and misremember it, as will I. We will talk the sea into submission.

EIGHT

The student only turned to Sartre as a last resort. The conventional advice he'd received was utterly useless. Years later, Sartre confessed a belief that the student had already made the decision before he came to him for advice. In a sense, that's *why* the student came to him. He made, Sartre said, exactly the decision that he'd predicted. This is all we know.

Another French philosopher and man of action, though a happier soul, was Maurice Merleau-Ponty. A friend of Sartre, he also fought against Germany as second lieutenant. Together with Simone de Beauvoir, Sartre and others, Merleau-Ponty founded the influential political journal *Les Temps Modernes* (over which he and Sartre eventually fought and split – as editors and friends). Like Sartre, he was inspired to write his main treatise during the heady months of 1945. Another tome, *Phenomenology and Perception*.

In it, Merleau-Ponty deals with the problem Descartes posed by pointing to sexual reproduction as evidence of a real, physical world. For it is only through sexual interaction that physical bodies can give birth to new minds. Not just that body precedes mind, but that *bodies* precede mind. Not just "I think therefore I am", but rather "I think therefore we are."

He continued the phenomenologist's project, but with a twist, arguing for the primacy of our bodies in perception. Reading Husserl, Heidegger and Sartre, one is left with the impression of the mind as an ethereal cloud looking out at the external world as if from behind a lens. But our knowledge of the world comes through bodily perception, from infancy onwards. By trying and testing the world with our mouth, eyes, hands, feet, our body and mind work together to gain an optimal grip on reality.

Through proprioception – the instinctive knowledge of whether our legs are crossed, whether our hands are open or fisted, how hard we need to throw a basketball to make it reach the basket – we can access alternative kinds of knowledge ignored by other philosophers. Through perceiving ourselves as spatially oriented in the physical world we can immediately and instinctively solve the famous Fr Ted Paradox: that "these are small, but the ones out there are far away". The body "skilfully copes" within a world that is "a field of significance organized by and for beings like us with our bodies, desires, interests, and purposes."[1]

Sartre's notion of freedom and choice posits a world in which the mind is independent and free, the great dictator of the body, instructing it to do this or that. But as much as the mind feels ethereal when dealing with theoretical questions, it is bound by its physicality.

BRENDAN MAC EVILLY

The things we put into our body – like coffee or drugs – or the things we put our body into – like the sea – determine the content, shape and flow of our thoughts and perceptions. And so physical activity shapes mental responses. The body's submersion in cold water releases endorphins, sends signals to the brain; the brain is forced rather than chooses to react as it does. Extreme stimuli create extreme responses. Equally, the aesthetic quality of the external world affects the shape and content of our mind in profound ways.

NINE

One night in late February, I lie awake in bed. I think about the different states of being. First, bed-existence: a near perfect physical comfort. There is little or no stimulus, just womb-warmth and darkness. In this state, the mind exits the physical world, drifts forward and backward in time, roams into pasts and futures where it cultivates fantasies and fears. This is sometimes a pleasure, but oftentimes it turns to unwelcome circular ruminations of real-life problems that cannot be solved here and now. The lack of physical stimulus can offer more freedom for the mind than is good for it.

Compare this to running-existence. Running incites a greater focusing of the mind, on the immediate obstacles at hand. The constant need to look at where your feet are landing, not to step in shit, to think only so far ahead as the pedestrian you're about to pass. Just as in meditation, there is a focus on breathing, reflection on your physical status: a twitch in the knee, aching in a shoulder perhaps. Running-existence is a meditation of sorts, but the mind's focus falls on the all-too-boring objects of consciousness.

Whereas sea-existence is something else entirely – a kind of nothing-being. It is not Husserl's intentional being, focused on the objects of consciousness. There is none of Heidegger's directedness towards the future. None of the anxiety of being *à la* Sartre, continually confronted by choice, or the freedom – the imperative even – to be other than what one is now.

I am just a few feet from shore, but the effortless suspension in water has an alien quality. There is a heightened awareness of my body and the freedom it enjoys, immersed in the physicality of the world yet relieved of the standard terrestrial restriction of gravity. I hang in suspension.

Floating like this provides all the results of meditation but without the effort of focusing the mind on one thing, or on nothing. The cold sensation from the water and the mesmeric vision of undulating sea hold our attention, giving an intense immediacy to our existence. In this state it is the body which drifts, not the mind. There is no musing on projects or plans, only the unfolding of the present moment. As Joyce says, "There is not past, no future; everything flows in an eternal present."

Yet it was a twenty-eight-day project that has led to this projectless headspace. To live authentically, we must accept that even our projects are pointless, yet joyful. Arbitrary, yet purposeful. Ultimately meaningless, yet meaningful to us. All of us have to bridge two truths, that there is no given meaning to life, nothing in the fabric of the world which shows or tells us how to live, yet at every turn we choose a path with a sense of purpose. And if we choose in accordance with our true instincts, impulses and desires, responding honestly to our unique situation, then our existence can feel authentic, meaningful, even *freu*.

[1] H. L. Dreyfus. *On the Internet*. (Routledge, 2001), p.26

BRENDAN MAC EVILLY

David Ishaya Osu

Dreaming

One broken night left
in a landscape, *velvet*—gone

are no winds, *glissando*—count
all the swans you see

and their shadows, *unison*—mute
and rum says the dreaming

there is a door, *clockwise*—new
leaves and the vine you want

to touch your own heart, *mirror*—a
glisten of henna to wake up to

Cherry Smyth

Lie Flat

Where branches were cut, dark nodes give
scar history to a wooden floor. I lie down,
outline them with my fingertip –

the whorl of skin learning the whorl of knots,
the open and closed rings that sound
stories of living and its wounds –

the places that we carry where forgiveness
jammed, like a crystal holed up in a muscle
that circling touch works free.

I think of the Chinese word for opting out –
tangping, which means "lie flat", refuse to be
rolled up in the tight race to the top.

The young are reversing the dream,
going to where trees grow, to breathe
leaf-breath. This cheered me today,

like the news from the North, that enemies
will sit together, share their words
for woods, their plans for planting;

and the new recruit in prison for saying no
to killing, who was spat on, and on release
will refuse again and be jailed again.

The olive branch is snapped
but the trunk records where it once grew
and birds still loop looking for their nest.

Michael Goodfellow

Named Storms

You told the season by what we did to water.
We tapped maple and drank what gathered.
Then nights were about metal:
brass spile, pail and handle
and what we added to the heated pot:
ground coffee and nettle,
wild mushrooms dried last summer. Rushing,

it gapped the still ground. In river mud
we picked soft pieces of ship wood,
from the salt, pegs in their worn holes.
When we oiled the wood the pegs swelled.

In the yard, we dug smooth stones
from when this was the riverbed—
fossil of movement, something swept over.

When the hurricane and surge
the brook flowed backward.
For days after, the well held the storm's salt.
Salt meant you couldn't tell the difference
between dew and frost, rain or snow.
Colour blindness for water.
For what time did to wanting.

The culvert churned and boiled,
tannin the brown-black of negatives.
Like a flood, you pointed the lens.

Then we loved what pooled.
In winter, ice clung to alder
but that was just another form of light.

Chimezie Chika

Against the Weather

My mother is a windmill in a whirlwind.
    – Chinua Ezenwa-Ohaeto

I

Even now, whenever I find myself caught by a random rain in the street, I still remember the dripping wet humiliation of that day in 2015 when I arrived in Owerri from Onitsha and trekked for hours in a blinding heavy rain from Control to my lodgings near IMSU Junction, clutching a black backpack. I had lost the money my mother had given me to an unknown pickpocket on the bus, and since it was already 7.00 p.m. when I arrived in the city, I essayed bravely into that rain and began to trek, forgetting in the swirling stress of my situation that I had a laptop in my backpack, and the laptop got soaked beyond remedy in the ensuing bath. Once I was on the road, the rain came at me from all directions and I was drenched in no time. For much of the trek I could hardly see the treacherous road before me, and I stumbled many times on the sloshy asphalt. And in the middle of it all, driven half-mad by the torrent in my ears, I thought I had come to the end of my days.

Shivering in my cold room later that night, I did not think about the possibility of having caught a cold. I only thought of the empty malt and beer cans my mother had gathered and sold to get the three thousand naira she'd given me. I could not possibly tell her what had happened—not against the knowledge of her daily exertions to make money despite the incessant waist pain she complained of, not against the knowledge of her failing business as a food vendor, not against the strain of the ever-looming apartment rent breathing down our necks. And so the semester stretched out before me like a desert. Yet I had to be in school somehow; I was the hope of my family.

That semester, I found that the only way I could get at least one meal every day was to stick to my female friends: there was Amaka, there was

Favour, and there was Dexterous. Amaka was by my side all through my second year in Imo State University, and many people thought we were dating. We'd walk to the lecture halls together, often sit together and go together to the cafeterias, where Amaka always paid for our meals. Sometimes we'd sit outside under one of the ubiquitous frangipanis that flanked the campus roads and the sides of the buildings, talking idly about our families. Amaka was one of the youngest of her siblings and sometimes, listening to her talking, I felt a persistent tug of melancholy, as if she desperately needed our companionship. What I saw in Amaka— what endeared her to me—was her resemblance to my mother, in the unforced, unstated way she cared about me.

There is a photo of my mother in the family album; it is small and seems to have been taken by the 'wait and take' Polaroid camera that was popular in Nigeria in the 1980s. Standing in a red-tinged studio room, my mother is young here: in her early twenties, fresh from the ungovernable mysteries of her teens. She is wearing a white and black circular-patterned wrapper with red cones in the black circles, a white pearl necklace and a gold wristwatch. In her beautiful face, full black hair, and dusty sandals, there is the light of a woman sure of her own lush prospects. How has the future turned out for her? The easy birth of twins, my brother and me, was a gift. Nothing else would matter for her in the end, if her boys succeeded. But was I fulfilling my promise in my first two years at university?

It was the constant hot emptiness in my belly and the unbearable thought of my mother's sadness which forced me into the examination hall of a GST course. I had agreed to take the exam for a student in the History Department, and he was to pay me seven thousand naira—a small sum by any stretch, but I was dizzy with desperation. He paid me half of the money and I entered the exam hall hoping to finish quickly. I managed to answer all the questions in forty minutes, but when I stood to submit my answer sheet, it started pouring outside and I could not leave the hall. I went back to my seat and waited, listening to the low murmur of students soliciting answers from their neighbors and watching the few heads bent in concentration. I looked up after a while and saw one of the invigilators standing beside me.

"You have finished?"

"Yes," I said, trying to calm my trembling limbs.

"That is good. What's your department?"

"English," I said without thinking.

"There is no English here. Are you not in the wrong hall?"

"Sorry sir. I mean History. I was lost in thought."

"You were lost in thought and forgot your department? Be careful."

I waited, choking with dread, but he turned and left, leaving me gasping for air.

II

I remember Mummy cooking onugbu soup when I was six. It was raining and Daddy had just returned from one of his trips. Whenever Daddy came back, Mummy would go to Ochanja Market and buy a sack of groundnuts and, over the next few weeks, she would cook them for us and sell the remnant in her kiosk downstairs, beside the gate of our three-story tenement building. That day, my twin brother Ebuka and I, and my younger sister, Chiamaka, sat in the parlor with Daddy watching a movie about a malevolent orca whale, while the noises and smells of Mummy's cooking—the pounding of the mortar, the clatter of Tupperware, the smell of ogiri and ugba—filtered in from the kitchen. After a time I got up, pricked by guilt, and stood by the kitchen door watching Mummy, but she shooed me away: "Go and watch film with your Daddy, nna."

When it rained heavily on the weekends, Daddy and Mummy would stay all day in their room, except when Daddy came out to watch the NTA News at 9 with Cyril Stober. I remember my mother's face, her cheeks curving constantly with laughter. In the days when Daddy was away, hauling tons of imported goods in his trailer from the ports in Lagos to locations all over the country, Mummy kept our routine going. She'd wake early to prepare our breakfast and school lunches; but there was always, in her slow deliberate manner, the anxious stasis of waiting.

I remember December of the year 2000, deep in the dry season, when Daddy killed a goat. We hadn't gone to our hometown, Umuaka, to spend the holidays, as many Nigerians do during Christmas. Onitsha was almost half empty and many of our fellow tenants in the tenement had traveled to their villages. The sky was stark and open, and the harmattan air was so cold that we put Vaseline on our lips and heels to keep them from cracking. That morning my twin and I followed Daddy downstairs to the back of our tenement to roast the goat in a big bonfire. As the yard filled with the acrid stench of burning animal hair, Daddy used a machete to scrape the burnt hair off the goat's body; its petrified head tilted to one side, the mouth open, showing a bizarre cluster of large teeth arranged in something like a sardonic smile. We ate a lot of meat that Christmas and Daddy gave some to the co-tenants who were still around. How fast days like these slip into the sibylline realm of memory, recalled only years later in lacerating moments of despair and shame.

III

Remember Onitsha in the early 2000s. The Bakassi vigilante group that administered jungle justice on criminals, under the authority of the state government; any sign of their fast onuazu bus or their red and black uniforms always sent people into convulsions of fear. Remember the rampant rumors of the Bakassi's spiritual powers used for detecting criminals; remember, too, the chaos of burning human bodies in tires that sent tall black palls of smoke up into the sky. Remember the coming of mobile phones, how Daddy bought a heavy Sony Ericsson with a flip that covered its keyboard, how he later bought Mummy a Motorola, the one everyone called 'Motorola egghead'; the phone booths that sprang up everywhere with their bright yellow and red umbrellas, selling recharge cards and offering call services for twenty naira, so that people who couldn't afford to buy the exorbitant phones could make calls.

Remember the record shops that played makossa and 'Danfo Driver' and 'African Queen,' and the young men that sagged their jean trousers, walking with a newfound swagger gleaned from American hip-hop. Remember the home movies that everyone watched. In the streets: fences, walls, and electric poles plastered with Nollywood movie posters; the film-for-hire shops that sprang up everywhere, sometimes two to three shops competing for customers on the same street. Were we overwhelmed by all the new things and events and sensations? What did we see, what did we make of all that tumult?

Remember how Mummy left her wooden kiosk and acquired a unit in a mechanics' workshop on the expressway to Awka, beside the Chukwudi Filling Station. There, she sold alcohol, cigarettes, jollof rice, and egg rolls. She'd leave very early, around 7.30 or 8.00 a.m., and come back around 7.00 p.m. Remember how Daddy traveled to the village and brought back two relatives to live with us, so we wouldn't be alone after school or during the long weekends. Do you remember how one of them, Chinelo, used to tell folktales deep into the night while we lay on mats in the parlor, fascinated?

Even if you don't remember much, you must remember that day, in early 2006, when Mummy came back and told us the engine of Daddy's trailer had failed. "We will manage from now on," she said, because Daddy would have no money to spare until he could afford a new engine. Standing in the corridor in the last light of the day, with our faces half-obscured by the approaching darkness, we all fell silent as if we had just been told that someone had died. I do not remember a lot from that day; the mind tends to erase such details. It is mostly my sister's yellow face that I see now, squatting near the door in that monkish way of hers, and it is her burst of tears that I hear. But Mummy paid our school fees that term, and we did not *manage*.

IV

How could we have known that we were at a crossroads, seen the sudden plunge ahead into dust and grit? Difficulty came gradually through the mid-2000s. Daddy's trailer suffered many issues, and so much of the money he made went to mechanics. But the vehicle was incessant: if it was not the engine today, it would be the gearbox and alternator or axle tomorrow. Mummy declared that our enemies were after us and dragged us to church crusades on Friday nights, where Daddy—wonder of wonders!—sometimes joined us. Mummy also joined a women's prayer group that met every Wednesday morning. The leader was a prophetess, and she told Mummy that enemies were after her husband because they wanted to take him, the same way they had taken all his siblings before their time.

It rained heavily the night before the news came. And because it had rained the day before, that day—the 6th of June 2008—was cold. It was a brooding day and heavy gray clouds amassed in the sky; the oblique rain persisted all day. Around 3.00 p.m., after a messenger informed Mummy of the tragedy, she left the house and started walking. She did not say anything to anyone. She faced northward and walked for nearly two miles, as she told me years later, then turned back. I remember seeing her crossing the corridor and going towards their room, still not talking, her yellow face round and puffy. In the days that followed, her face grew puffier as her body shed weight. There was a rupture in the sinew of the world and it drained the mother I knew; in her place there was only a weary figure withering with something hidden and unutterable.

I was also buried in sorrow to a certain extent, but I had no tears to show for it like my mother and siblings. I had not allowed myself to unravel all that was happening; my emotions remained frozen for a long time, like permafrost. Not knowing how to deal with my mother in my dry-eyed agitation, I was thankful when relatives arrived to take control of everything.

V

When I think of my mother before my father's death, I remember one song she loved and played a lot in the late '90s and early 2000s: Chaka Chaka's 'Umqombothi.' She said she stopped playing the song because it reminded her of things she wanted to forget. Its lyrics, that had evoked hope and relaxation for her, now brought only fear and loathing; loathing of death and fear of a feckless future without a partner. I see those wet weeks in June clearly now: my mother convulsing in their room, her voice shattering the silence; the thrashing and the screaming; the journey to the village, with my half-brother Obinna, my father's first son, driving us. The confusing days that followed; the hundreds of mourners from all over the country, badgering us—all six of Daddy's children from his two wives—with glowing condolences. But amidst all this my mother sat there in the front of the house beside her co-wife, our senior mother Helen, their hair completely shaved in the customary mourning of widows. And in the redness of my mother's eyes, there seemed to be an edginess lurking. What could it be? What anger and what frustration? What pain and what endurance? What love and what loneliness? A thought passed through my mind then: was there a possibility that this was all a bad dream?

The dry season that year, which was supposed to hold sway by November, turned out to be strange. Clouds crowded the borderless sky. In confusion, the rain came down. Trees dripped blobs of water. Pools formed watery mirrors in the rutted earth. And there were no dry, cold winds whooshing through desolate streets and village paths, scorching grasses, forcing the trees to shed their dry leaves, cracking lips and heels, rousing dust clouds like spirits invoked from the depths of the earth. Perhaps the biggest realization for a young man is that life contains scarce certainties. There is no script, no scope. Only the tips and turns of random events. He discovers that what we call life is an act of striving against the vagaries of the weather, against the ever-looming possibility of storms.

In the second semester of my second year at university, Blessing, one of my classmates, lost her mother. As is usually done in such situations, the entire class contributed money for Blessing and hired a bus to take us to her hometown in Awgu, where the burial was being held. It was a long winding road from Owerri to Awgu through three states—Imo, Abia, and Enugu. Sitting by the window, I had a good view of the places we passed. From Okigwe onwards the landscape became hilly, and only grew more rugged as the old bus strained through the slopes of Awgu's fog-covered highlands. Looking out the window, we gasped at the narrow path we were traveling, thousands of feet above sea level with sharp cliffs on one side and a dense forest below. It seemed to me, then, that in undertaking a perilous journey to pay respects to the dead, we might see ourselves on the wrong side of life. It is this intense awareness of our final and necessary end that keeps us all rushing to finish this and that thing—it is this awareness that makes the idea of milestones possible: birthdays, graduations, marriages, promotions, awards. And yet, not many of us are prepared when the end comes. I have tried to think about my mother's death, and though I know that life coalesces towards it, nothing will ever prepare me.

VI

A rage smoldered inside my heart for a long time. There seemed to be no end to the desperation, the scrounging, the strife, the shame. What had been hope after my father's burial became isolation. There was no response from Obinna, who had taken initial responsibility for the family. There was no one anywhere; only us. My mother's restaurant business, which had moved from the Awka/Onitsha expressway to our street, shut down, because it had come to a point where only one or two customers would come each day. She began petty trading with women in the surrounding rural towns. She'd wake up early, around 5.30 a.m., go to Odekpe or Umueri to purchase whatever was available—vegetables and dried meat mostly—and sell it at Ose Market. She came back one day and said a man had slapped her for blocking the road with her wares. I trembled with fury. "Bia gosi m nwoke a," I said, standing up quickly and moving towards the door. "Let it go, nna," she said, "O ife a na-afu n' uwa." And then later she started selling food in a wheelbarrow, pushing it all over our neighborhood.

I gained admission to Imo State University in 2013 and, with the help of my maternal uncles, managed to pay my acceptance fee. My mother gave me some foodstuffs and off I went to school with little else except the paltry amount I had saved from teaching extramural classes for senior secondary school students. Without money or accommodation, I suffered greatly in my first three months, sleeping in empty classroom halls and washing in the bathrooms of hostels nearby. I went around

Owerri every day looking for part-time jobs that came with some sort of accommodation—the sun hot and spiky on the back of my neck, the glass-and-concrete façades of the buildings stiff and insular—but found none. The few places I could find wanted full-time workers, which was no fit for me because I wanted to remain in school.

Lying on the hard bench of the empty ETF II hall at night, the cold draught from the windows assaulting my ribs so that I could not breathe from the pain, I worried that I might not ever be able to pay for a hostel, and then I worried for my life. But each somber morning I rose, prepared, and went to school, and in the afternoon continued my job-hunting. While passing a building site one day, I asked the manager if I could work there, and he agreed. Very early the next morning I was already at the site, carrying cement blocks up to the third decking, where the masons were laying the walls. Towards evening, as I tried to negotiate my way up the stairs carrying a heavy block on my head, I fell and bruised my left knee, shoulders and arms. And I just lay there among the broken blocks and residues of old cement, too fatigued to examine my wounds.

Those who knew me during my first year at IMSU would remember that I always carried a heavy black backpack, but none of them would have known that bag contained all my worldly possessions. I carried it wherever I went in those early months in Owerri. On a whim, I switched my small Nokia phone off and refused to call home. Why add to my mother's struggles? I was only in school so her life would be better. But each new day my drab reality taunted this belief, and my ardent dreams of setting my mother up in a nice house one day seemed to be dissipating.

There is a sense in which the simplicity of privation confers a certain beatific aura on the poor, so that people begin to facetiously admire what they call their *resilience*. The Bedouins have lived in the desert for centuries, having turned one of Earth's harshest environments into a place for a noble life, so that featureless stretches of undulating sand dunes, light brown camels, tall date palms, and the clear waters of a guelta become idyllic to the outsider. But all Lawrence of Arabia wannabes will soon find out that there is nothing romantic about a landscape whose very constitution is against human life. All that time I had given myself up completely to a frugal way of living, while making sure I remained as physically presentable as possible, and I always found it amusing that some classmates thought I was employed and busy, with no time for frivolities. But I woke one morning, in March 2014, weak and unable to get up. I switched on my phone and sent a brief text to Obinna's old number, though I was not sure if it was still in use; I told him I was now a student at IMSU and needed somewhere to stay.

What kept me moving in the torrid despair of my freshman year was denial. I still believed, with irrational conviction, that after nearly six years my father would return. In the middle of the second semester, I decided to go home. My sister was the only one there when I arrived that Saturday. I asked about Mummy and she replied that our mother was at the market and would soon return. Ebuka had gone to watch a Premier League match at a viewing center on the next street. I sat in the parlor in silence, my sister's eyes moving curiously over me. I ignored her. The sofas seemed to have grown very old in my time away, their red coverings torn in places, the yellowed foam peeking out. The old National television on the cabinet no longer worked, so there was nothing else to do. I had dozed off when Mummy came back. When she woke me, I stood and hugged her despite my shock. She looked emaciated, and her skin had darkened unevenly with sunburn. I opened my mouth to say something, but no words came.

"We tried to reach you, nna. We called everybody. Look how thin you are."

I looked from her burnt face to her faded dress, unable to say anything.

"Why didn't you call us? What happened?"

I looked around the parlor without seeing anything, then I looked upwards at the white ceiling, then I sat down on the sofa and broke down in tears.

VII

Another memory of that Saturday comes. The mind makes an effort to forget but the memory has latched onto a feeling and has refused to let go. A strong wind is blowing outside; there is shouting. My mother goes to the balcony to gather the clothes spread out on the iron railing. I follow her. Leaning on the railing, I watch the trees bending, people running, chickens squawking with trepidation, the rusty zinc roofs of the older houses clapping in the wind. The wind buffets my mother's loose scarf, inflating it with air. The dust rises, a door slams somewhere in another flat within the tenement, the aroma of oha soup floats up. An ancient longing overwhelms me. I long for the gathering clouds and the coming rain; I long for serene mornings and quiet evenings; I long for the freedom of plenty and the clarity of sated hunger; I long for my mother's full cheeks and for the groundnuts and rich soups of the old days; I long for the heat of being alive; I long for far-flung places, wet hills, dry valleys, green plains, the imaginative reaches of places I have read in books and seen in videos; I long for sunny days, wet days, and cool days. I long to strain my soul against the elements, to be alive without the fear and loathing of the unknown.

Jo Bear

Persephone in Éire

Again, I wake recalling humus & stringy roots
      flossed through my canines. When I eat

of the earth I recall the cleaving of seasons
      in my chest. A miracle: in myth as in memory

nothing is certain. At night every dream is a mother
      threshing wheat to hold back the solstice.

By her hands might a body grow taproots
      against wind over the longest days,

against underground countries floored in green.
      I, wandering heart, back facing dawn,

paean of the lengthening shadow. It was not
      for a man but the verdancy of the hills

he made that I stayed. Forgive me, love,
      for the body I have forgotten beside

the hearth & the frost under my nails. On the surface
      of the river are six seeds. Come spring,

I will describe to mouths that have never hungered
      the flavor of ripe fruit. A list of all I cannot

hold: blackcurrants, your hipbones, the breaking
      heat. There is a bog under your ribs

where the relief of me waits for flesh to follow.
     Your breath is the weather of this land,

your temples silk & salt. I tell my mother
     I'll be home soon & spend the nights

smudging the horizon line with a careful thumb
     until it bursts open. Until it shatters.

I do not remember if hunger or girl became me first,
     remember only your harvest & my open mouth.

Jo Bear

Gentrification Ghazal

By the bridge, the crane chooses to peck apart the city,
its stilted knees feign interest in the shape of the city.

For a week, I live on a friend's floor & gnaw gratitude down
to gristle. Down each lane is an empty house because of the city.

I shop above where Vikings clutched antlered creatures
close to the manes of their chests before there was a city.

You kiss me in the kitchen of every ruined apartment I flee
& your tongue has the grain of a closed door in the city.

I learn the country's sweat. I learn when the bombs made a rush
hour carrion stain, what the rain hides. I cannot call it mine, this city.

In their hunger, gulls pluck crumbs from the sky & children tell
their parents in vain that stars are being disappeared in the city.

We go to the sea & I am promised to another country. In the wind,
your hair is a swirling vane & this too is the sheer cliffs of the city.

Begin again, remind me of the euphony of the streets after school,
the children & the joints they sprained in haste to join the city.

A country is the grinding of molars, is a waning moon. The bank
asks where I can claim my mail. I tell them the name of the city.

Paula Dias Garcia

a thing that growls and moans both

a heart is
a complicated beast
but it's also
very simple

all the time it wants
and sometimes
it has

and I've nothing to add
that hasn't been said by
the poets the laureates my
betters

except how it lies softly
on my chest
both a blanket and a
weight

James Owens

One Year After a Summer of Fires

Sleepers dream of cool hands soothing fever.
At dawn, rain washes light down to the dim street,
where no one walks yet, and over houses
and yards, and brushes it onto the leaves
of the lilacs by the fence, which gleam now,
as if renewing their naive project of life,
while the first, wandering tendrils of rainwater
swell the dry roots of sunflowers to sleekness.

How many stories begin "at daybreak, the rain ..."?
Yet, this is the story we have, and the person
at the open window, wakened by soft thunder
and watching the still empty street gather
its brightening, shapeless puddles, must tell it.

Outside the spared town, mist curls up
where rain sighs in the grass. On blackened earth,
tender weeds and brambles have knitted over ash.
Woven nests wake among the saplings,
and sheltered birds rouse to pip and rustle.
Seeds from cones that burst in heat are sprouting,
as happens after a burn—always, so far.

Notes on Contributors

Christine Barkley is an Irish-American writer based in the Pacific Northwest. Her poems and essays can be found in *The Yale Review*, *The Manhattan Review*, *The Journal*, *The Massachusetts Review*, *Salamander*, and *The Missouri Review*, among others. She is a poetry reader for *TriQuarterly* and *The Maine Review*.

Jo Bear is a poet, scholar, and educator currently pursuing their MFA in poetry at North Carolina State University. Their poetry appears or is forthcoming in *West Branch*, *The South Carolina Review*, *Blue Earth Review*, *Poetry Ireland Review*, *ROPES Literary Journal*, and elsewhere.

Annette C. Boehm (she/they) is a queer, Autistic writer and the author of two collections: *The Knowledge Weapon* and *The Apidictor Tapes*. Their poems can be found in *Room*, *Poetry*, *South Dakota Review*, *The Banshee*, and other places.

Rebecca Bratten Weiss is an editor and journalist residing in rural Ohio, U.S.A. Her poems have appeared in numerous publications, as well as three chapbook collections, most recently *The Gods We Have Eaten* (Bottlecap Press, 2023).

Diarmuid Cawley is from Sligo, Ireland. His poems have featured in *The Martello*, *The Belfast Review*, *Trasna*, *Smashing Times*, *Unapologetic Mag*, *Moonstone Press*, *Guzzle Magazine*, *The Honest Ulsterman*, *Poetry as Commemoration*, *Channel* and *Howl*. He is working on his first collection.

Helen Chen (she/they) is a Chinese-American writer based in New York City. She is working towards a degree in English and Creative Writing at Columbia. Helen received the Richmond B. Williams Traveling Fellowship to study postcolonial Singaporean literature. Her work has been featured in *JMWW*, *The Citron Review*, *J Journal*, and others. She was a finalist for the Ned Vizzini Prize, Iridescence Awards, and *The Lumiere Review*

Writing Contest, selected by Elaine Hsieh Chou. She is curious about characters and her grandma's scarf.

Chimezie Chika is an Igbo writer of fiction and nonfiction. His works have appeared in or are forthcoming from, amongst other places, *The Republic*, *Terrain.org*, *Efiko Magazine*, *Dappled Things*, and *Afrocritik*. A Runner-Up for the 2023 J.F. Powers Prize for Short Fiction, he has received fellowships from the LLEAA (2024) and the Ebedi Residency (2021).

Gemma Cooper-Novack's debut poetry collection *We Might As Well Be Underwater* (Unsolicited Press, 2017) was a finalist for the CNY Book Award. She's published chapbooks with Warren Tales and The Head & the Hand. Her poetry and fiction have appeared in more than forty journals; her plays have been produced across the United States. Gemma was a winner of Syracuse University's 2023 All University Doctoral Prize for her hybrid poetic dissertation exploring the writing lives of LGBTQ+ teenagers.

Paula Dias Garcia is a queer writer from Brasília, MA in Creative Writing from the University of Limerick. Their works include poetry and short fiction in *Analog Science Fiction & Fact*, *Crest Letters*, *The Ogham Stone*, *Silver Apples* and *Riverbed Review*. Currently, they're the artistic director for Sans. PRESS.

Daniel Fuller is a British and Irish writer of poetry and fiction. His work has been published in *The North*, *The Stinging Fly*, and *The Madrigal*. Though born in England, he is now based in Oslo, Norway where he spends his time obsessing over language, decolonisation and "beloved community."

Robert René Galván, born in San Antonio of Indigenous/Mexican heritage, resides in New York City where he works as a professional musician and poet. His collections of poems include *Meteors*, *Undesirable: Race and Remembrance*, Somos en Escrito Foundation Press, *Standing Stones*, Finishing Line Press, and *The Shadow of Time*, Adelaide Books.

Michael Goodfellow is the author of the poetry collections *Naturalism, An Annotated Bibliography* (2022) and *Folklore of Lunenburg County* (2024), both published by Gaspereau Press, and his poems have appeared in the *Literary Review of Canada*, *The Dalhousie Review*, and elsewhere. He lives in Nova Scotia.

Ellen Harrold (She/Her) is an Irish artist and writer as well as editor-in-chief of *Metachrosis Literary*. She uses drawing, text, and textiles to explore physics, anatomy, and ecology through creative abstraction. She has published poetry in English and Irish in magazines such as *Shearsman*, *Causeway / Cabhsair*, and *Skylight 47*.

Anastasia Jill (they/them) is a queer writer living in Central Florida. They have been nominated for Best American Short Stories, The Pushcart Prize, and several other honors. Their work has been featured or is upcoming with *Poets.org*, *Sundog Lit*, *Flash Fiction Online*, *Contemporary Verse 2*, *Broken Pencil*, and more.

Louise Kim is an undergraduate student at Harvard University. Their Pushcart Prize- and Best of the Net-nominated writing has been published in a number of publications, including *Frontier Poetry*, *Chautauqua Journal*, and *Panoply Zine*. Her debut poetry collection, *Wonder is the Word*, was published in May 2023.

Hannah Linden, from Devon, UK, won the Café Writers Poetry Competition 2021, was Highly Commended for the Wales Poetry Award 2021 and came second in the Leeds Peace Poetry Prize 2024. Her debut pamphlet, *The Beautiful Open Sky* (V. Press), was shortlisted for the Saboteur Award for Best Poetry Pamphlet 2023. X: @hannahl1n

Brendan Mac Evilly is the author of *At Swim: A Book About the Sea* (2016, Collins Press). He runs *Holy Show* arts magazine and production house, and runs the National Mentoring Programme on behalf of the Irish Writers Centre. His debut novel *Deep Burn* is forthcoming with Marrowbone Books in 2025.

David Mullin is an archaeologist and writer based in West Yorkshire. He is returning to poetry after a career in academia and is currently writer in residence at the Special Collections at the University of Bradford, working on a project focused on the poetry of archaeologist Jacquetta Hawkes.

Is file agus scríbhneoir aiteach agus tras é Keev Ó Baoill (siad/é) atá bunaithe i mBaile Átha Cliath. Beidh a phaimfléad dar teideal *the end of the fucking world / shitty airport poems* foilsithe le Back Room Poetry i mí na Samhna, 2024. Tá a chuid scríbhneoireacht foilsithe in *Channel*, *Back Room Poetry*, *Vernacular Journal*, *Gnashing Teeth Mag*, *Powders Press*, *Ache Magazine* agus in áiteachaí eile. Is féidir teacht ar Keev @keevobaoill ar Twitter agus Instagram.

Keev (Boyle-Darby) Ó Baoill (they/he) is a trans, Irish poet and writer. His upcoming chapbook *the end of the fucking world / shitty airport poems* is due to be published by Back Room Poetry in November 2024. Keev is Co-founder of *tinycrowdcollective* (@tinycrowdzine), a queer, trans-led zine looking to capture moments of intensity, banality, and everything in between. Their work has been published by *Channel*, *Gnashing Teeth*, *Vernacular Journal*, *Back Room Poetry*, *Powders Press*, *SEXTANT*, *GCN*, *The Places Zine* and *Ache Magazine* among others. You can find them and their work on socials (@keevobaoill) or at linktr.ee/kvrbyrl.

Frances Ogamba is a 2024 Jacobson Scholar at the Hawkinson Foundation for Peace and Justice. She received the 2024 Walter H. Judd Travel fellowship, the 2024 Graduate Summer Support Fellowship, and the 2022 College of Liberal Arts fellowship from the University of Minnesota, Twin Cities.

Tess O'Regan is a writer from Cork with a degree in Film and English Literature from UCC, whose writing engages ideas of time, gender, and liminality. She was previously highly commended by the Eoin Murray Memorial Scholarship in creative writing. Her work can be found on the scholarship's website.

David Ishaya Osu is a poet and street photographer living in South Australia, where he is completing a PhD in Creative Writing at the University of Adelaide.

James Owens' newest book is *Family Portrait with Scythe* (Bottom Dog Press, 2020). His poems and translations appear widely in literary journals, including recent or upcoming publications in *CV2*, *Arc*, *Dalhousie Review*, *Queen's Quarterly*, and *Atlanta Review*. He earned an MFA at the University of Alabama and lives in a small town in northern Ontario, Canada.

David Ralph's work has been published in *The Dublin Review*, *Banshee*, *Southword*, *Litro*, *Fish*, and *New Irish Writing*. He won a New Irish Writing Award in 2020. In 2021 he was a recipient of a place on the Words Ireland National Mentoring Programme. In 2022 he placed third in the Fish Memoir Prize.

Mandy Shunnarah (they/them) is an Appalachian and Palestinian-American writer who calls Columbus, Ohio, USA home. Their first book, *Midwest Shreds*, was released in 2024 from Belt Publishing, and their second book, a poetry collection titled *We Had Mansions*, is forthcoming from Diode Editions in 2025. Read more at mandyshunnarah.com.

Cherry Smyth is a poet, novelist, and art writer. She has published four poetry collections, *When the Lights Go Up*, *One Wanted Thing* (both Lagan Press), *Test, Orange* (Pindrop Press, 2012), and *Famished* (Pindrop Press, 2019). Her novel *Hold Still* was published by Holland Park Press, 2013. See www.cherrysmyth.com.

Fawn Emmalee Ward is an American author striving to create emotional work with a strong sense of place. Her work has been published or is forthcoming in *Meetinghouse Magazine*, *Pinhole Poetry*, *Variant Literature*, and *The Ghastling*. Fawn is also a Senior Editor for *Weird Lit Magazine*. Read more at fawnward.com.

Erin Wilson's poems have appeared in *The Honest Ulsterman*, *Manchester Review*, *Cordite Review*, *Grain*, *Verse Daily*, and elsewhere internationally. The title poem from her collection, *Blue*, won a Pushcart. She lives on Robinson-Huron Treaty Territory, in Northern Ontario, Canada. Her dearest friends are trees and wind, and wind through trees.

Thank you to our generous patrons

Hannah Gaden Gilmartin
Sara Nishikawa

We also want to thank those patrons who wish to remain anonymous.